BLINDED ME WITH SCIENCE

AN OPPOSITES ATTRACT COLLEGE ROMANCE

LESSON IN LOVE
BOOK TWO

TARA SEPTEMBER

ABOUT

Emerson is majoring in biology, so isn't it about time she got a real lesson in it?

Emerson Powers has been so focused on obtaining her science degree that she's neglected the more social aspects of college life. With the new start of her junior year, she's determined to fix that with a real hands-on lesson in biology. The assignment is simple enough—teach the rock star's son how to be good, while he shows her how to be very bad. Two objectives, one outcome … will the lesson be love or heartbreak?

Steel is no longer the bad boy Emerson knew from prep school, and he's set to prove it by helping Emerson complete her secret list of desired college experiences. And if he can convince her that they are meant to be together along the way, even better!

While teaming up on experiments, both in and out of the classroom, Emerson discovers a new side to Steel. Leaving her to question everything she thought she knew. Still, is it enough to forgive the past or just mere chemistry?

As they say, opposites attract like a magnet to steel, or in this case, Emerson to Steel.

EMERSON

"These are the best years of your life."

If one more adult tells me this, I'm going to flat-out scream. I can't even count how many times I heard this insipid platitude during my summer break, and now it's echoing around in my brain to taunt me on the first day of my junior year at Thatcher College.

Sure, my first two years here have been better than my prep school days being labeled the dean's off-limits, brainy daughter, but I'm hardly living my best life. I mainly study, eat junk food, and stream one series after another in my dorm room, sometimes with the occasional friend joining in. It's chill and I love being on my own, but I doubt it's what everyone is going on about when they refer to their glory days.

Hell, I haven't attended one campus party, never fooled around with some rando, or accomplished any other collegiate social milestone. Seriously, am I even a college student? I might as well have attended an online school and saved my parents the room and board fees.

Ugh!

My audible self-loathing is a little too loud, and I quickly glance around the classroom, which fortunately is still empty. Yup, just me and the overpowering smell of Clorox. I'm the only one here because you know my father has ingrained in me what Packers' Coach Vince Lombardi famously said, "If you are five minutes early, you are already ten minutes late."

So, here I am, almost twenty minutes ahead of time for Advanced Bio. Forever the goody-goody, I'm seated front row center in the auditorium-style setup with a brand-new set of colored gel pens, out and ready.

Not gonna lie. I've been stoked for this class, especially since it fulfills a double requirement. That's two objectives to cross off my course list to fulfilling my major in Biology with a Chem minor. I really wanted to take this class last year before Professor Sanger retired, but I guess so did every other sciencophile because I was wait-listed. Naturally, I already researched the new course leader, Dr. Albright, who hails from Stanford and has an impressive score on RankMyProfessors.com. Although, I didn't love seeing terms like "out-of-the-box" and "avant-garde" being praised in terms of her teaching style, but I suppose I'm here to try new things before I hopefully start my career, possibly as a biochemist or a chemical engineer.

But I should probably have a life before then too. I wouldn't want to look back a few years from now and be filled with regrets. I must, I repeat, *must* make the most of a new school year and thus, new start. But my time spent as a social outcast and being sheltered by my parents did not prepare me for the true life of a college student. I can see that now as clearly as glowing phosphorus. Yes, I need to truly experience college in all its aspects.

Flipping through my notebook to an open page near the back, I make a list of experiences to finally check off before the next summer break. This way, I can nod in agreement when someone wistfully informs me these are the best years of *my* life.

With a purple pen, I write down: "I solemnly swear that I am up to no good." I smile seeing my geeky headline for this new list. Potterhead for life, baby! Yikes, I might need to tone down my fandom love if I'm going to accomplish any of these goals though.

1. Do something stupid (does this list count?)
2. Execute an epic prank (nothing mean!)
3. Go to a dance club (fake ID or wait till December?)
4. Attend a party on Greek row (invite needed?)
5. Get drunk (safely though.)
6. Hookup
7. ~~Make love~~ Have sex

I could keep going, but seven is a lucky number and I'll need some luck to, you know, get lucky. Seven is also an indivisible prime number, but I don't suppose that helps at all. Seven dwarves. Seven days in a week. Oh, and seven is the limit to the amount of information we can process and remember at one time. It's perfect! I reread my list, committing it to memory.

I feel better simply putting pen to paper and seeing my inner desires written out. After all, the first step to any action is planning, right? Besides, there hasn't been a list yet that I haven't completed … eventually, and I have one hundred seventy days to do it. I got this.

The creak of the classroom door opening has me slamming my notebook shut. A tall and buff, sandy-haired guy enters, and I can't help but stare. Enlisting the help of a frat brother like this specimen seems like the easiest solution to my list. He could probably help me cross off several experiences right off the bat, particularly the last four. And OMG, he looks perfect, but so does the girl on his arm. The couple head toward the very back row and proceed to make out. And why not? It's not like they even noticed my presence.

I sag in my chair. Right. The only way I can hang with a guy like that is if I tutor him in exchange or something. And how would that conversation even go? *"Excuse me, I'll help you get an A if you give me the D."* I cover my mouth to keep from laughing at my own joke but am still giggling inside. God, if only I had the balls to propose something like that.

After the entrance of the get-a-room couple, it's a steady stream of students filing in. Most I know, not all by name, but I recognize them from previous classes. My friend and study partner, Asif, gives me a wink as he climbs the steps past me, self-consciously smoothing out his dark mustache, which is new this year. I think it looks a bit much, but he seems awfully proud of it. Doesn't matter if I'm into it or not because I don't meet *his* sexual criteria of being another dude. Besides, considering he spends most of his Friday nights with us nerds ordering takeout, he'd probably have the same items to check off.

I give up looking at the door. Another science geek is unlikely to offer much aid anyway. I should just rip up this list and continue keeping on like I have been. Maybe my best years lie outside of college anyway.

A deep male voice cuts through my head trash. A very *familiar* male voice.

"If it isn't the First Kid."

No. Fucking. Way.

I take my time turning my head, dreading this unexpected reunion more than a root canal. Did my brief woe-is-me walk down high school outcast lane conjure him here to torture me in college now too?

Hoping this is a hallucination, I hesitantly cast my eyes up. But it's not a dream—it's a nightmare. Steely Nash, the son of famed alternative rock star Diesel, is standing before me as sexily rumpled as ever in tight, faded jeans and a vintage-looking, black T-shirt that clings to his pecs and ripped abs like a second skin. It probably costs more than my entire wardrobe too.

Forget the shirt. What in the hell is he doing here? Maine is as far from Los Angeles as you can get and one of the reasons why I chose this private, northeastern college to begin with. That and the scholarship they offered me. And why would "Steel," as he likes to go by, be taking a Bio 201 course? That would mean he'd have to have taken several science prerequisites first, and for some reason, that is what is blowing my mind right now, not the fact that I can still recognize his voice after a two-year absence. But really, he's never been far from my mind despite the miles I thought were separating us.

Like his name, his eyes are steel-colored and currently giving me a once-over, starting at the top of my head, stopping briefly to take in the pen sticking out of my messy bun since I couldn't find a hair tie when unpacking. His gaze ever so slowly lowers over my breasts, which feel unexpectedly heavy under his perusal, then all the way down to my tapping foot. I instantly stop the telltale nervous habit, but I fear I only called more attention to it. Dammit! I hope the jerking action at least hid the delicious tremble that shook through me following the same trail as his hooded gaze had traveled.

Pushing my glasses back up to the bridge of my nose, I finally find my tongue. "Steel," I say, my voice embarrassingly breathy as I continue to drink him in. His hair is dark, tousled, and ink black. It looks as soft as silk, and I almost sigh, longing to touch it.

"I guess I should say First Lady now," Steel amends with a devilish smile that has me sucking in for air, it's that stupidly powerful. "Wait, no," he hastens, adjusting the strap of his golden-brown, leather shoulder bag. "That makes it sound like you're married to your dad, and that's not what I meant. Ew, sorry! It's just that you look more mature now. But not in an old lady way either. Just, you no longer can be called kid, you know?"

He hurries on, shifting from foot to foot as I stare open-mouthed. I can't believe the self-assured Steely

Nash is appearing awkward for a change. Nervous even. He's acting like me, and for a moment, I feel sympathetic toward him, but then I remember who I'm talking to—the very guy who started my nickname "First Kid" back at Franklin Academy.

"You look great is what I meant to say," he finishes lamely, and I wonder why he's blowing smoke up my ass. I'm not left with much time to process all of this because Dr. Albright is standing in front of the room, addressing her class.

"Welcome, everyone, to Advanced Bio."

Steel drops into the seat next to me and extends his long legs out, taking up the empty space before him. He reminds me of a relaxed panther, waiting for prey to fall into his lap. Damned if I'll let it be me again.

So much for a new year and new freaking start!

2

—————

STEEL

To say Emerson is surprised to see me is an understatement. Actresses in slasher films have looked less horrified.

But I can understand her shock. After all, I already knew she was attending Thatcher and it's been a minute.

I shrug my shoulders. Not that I'm stalking her or anything. I was only curious to see where Emerson ended up post-graduation. If she was doing okay, stuff like that. It's how I learned about this hidden gem of a college in the first place. So yeah, I knew I'd likely see her eventually. Especially since earning a Bachelor of Science degree from Thatcher's business school requires additional mathematics and science courses, which has always been Emerson's thing.

Shaking my head, I steal a sideways glimpse. This girl … the only one who's made me want to be a better person. She changed my whole messed-up life and has no clue whatsoever. And from the way she's scrunching her pert nose and squinting her beautiful, blue eyes behind her glasses, she's not at all happy to see me. I don't blame her. In any case, I'm back now and she was going to have to deal with me.

Doesn't help that I totally just blew our first meeting again. My bad! But every witty line I'd ever rehearsed or imagined went straight out the window the moment she aimed her wide, blue eyes, as deep as any ocean, on me.

The all-too-seldom pictures she's posted over the years did nothing to prepare me for seeing real-life Emerson again. Her long, brown hair is in a cute knot on the top of her head, she has a sexy pair of black-rimmed glasses on, and all that covers that shapely body of hers is a teeny, cotton short set that shows off her smooth thighs and long legs. Put together, the ensemble is fucking adorable—and hot. I always considered Em an understated beauty, but now I don't know how to describe it. She seems more comfortable in her own skin, or something like that. What I *do* know is that being away from Franklin Academy and Los Angeles has done her good. Hell, it has for me too.

Our professor has been talking for a while but I haven't caught a word. If I'm going to show Emerson that I'm a changed man, not paying attention in class won't win me any points. I pull my laptop out from my satchel and open it up. I'm ready to be Mr. Diligent and listen intently to the quirky Dr. Albright, who is giving off a strong granola vibe. I peg her as someone who would not be impressed with the fact that I'm the son of Diesel.

I like her already.

"This year's seminar will consist of individual tests based on my lectures *and* monthly team projects, partner presentations, and joint essays, which will take up the other half of your grade," announces Dr. Albright, and the classroom groans, including Emerson. I think it sounds interesting though. "This means you will be paired up for the entire semester, and if your partner fails, your grades will suffer too. It's a symbiotic relationship."

Whoa, what now? The resulting uproar in the room is almost comical, as are the barrage of questions being aimed at the professor faster than the tempo of one of Diesel's rock ballads. A preppy-looking guy in the back, who'd been hooking up with a blonde beauty next to him, stands up and proclaims, "But I'm on the soccer team, so between practices and games, my schedule makes teamwork extremely difficult."

Dr. Albright smiles a little too sweetly. "Ironic that being on a team will affect your teamwork. As with evolution, you'll need to adapt to survive this class."

"Can we at least pick our partners?" he whines, his eyes practically bugging out of his head. This is obviously not a guy who's used to hearing the word no. I recline farther in my seat, enjoying the show. Oh yeah, I chose the right class.

"Sorry, but no," Dr. Albright states adamantly. "In the real world, you're going to have to work with people you might not mesh with. As you probably already know, there are five main symbiotic relationships: mutualism, commensalism, predation, parasitism, and competition. It's up to you guys to determine what kind of partnership yours will be, so I suggest you figure out how to coexist and bring out each other's strengths. Remember, rising tides lift all boats."

The murmurs and outbursts are growing louder. Dr. Albright is about to have a mob on her hands, but she's looking as unfazed as a divorce lawyer. "Don't worry," she calls out to the crowd, her smile never wavering. "You still have a week to drop this course without penalty."

Emerson's shocked inhale is louder than the one she released upon seeing me. I guess my presence is at least preferred over her dropping a course. Now I don't feel so bad. Kinda.

"But the best classes are filled by now," complains a female voice behind me, and I notice soccer dude collecting his stuff and tugging on his girlfriend's arm to leave. But she shakes her head and remains seated. Good for her.

"Let's begin," shouts Dr. Albright over the chaos, not bothering to answer any more questions. "Matching you to your partner is going to come down to biology, specifically genetics." Her announcement seems to give the mutiny pause. I know I'm curious.

"We'll start with sex."

Yup, definitely interested!

I sneak another sideways glance at Emerson. She's literally writing down everything that Dr. Albright is saying, and it takes every ounce of my willpower to keep from laughing out loud and teasing her for it. That's what the old Steely would do and it got me nowhere, particularly with a good girl like Emerson.

"Those with the XY chromosome, head to the back of the room and stand in a vertical row, side by side. XX chromosomes, come to the front by me and do the same."

Most of the students follow her command, but whiny soccer guy leaves, slamming the door behind him like a child's mid-temper tantrum. Good riddance.

Personally, I'm not happy having to separate from Emerson so soon, but she, on the other hand, is dashing away from me like her beakers have caught on fire. I climb the stairs, two at a time, and fill an empty space in the top row with the rest of the males. A skinny guy next to me with an impressive stache slaps me on the back like we're old friends, and I give him a nod, not wanting to appear rude. Who knows, he might end up being my partner for the semester. Knowing exactly who I'd rather be partnered up with, though, my gaze immediately finds Emerson, who is standing across the room at attention, ready and eager to follow the professor's next command.

"Now, on to inherited traits," Dr. Albright announces. "If you have curly hair, step forward." Eight people come forward from around the room. "Perfect, an even number. Whoever you are facing from the opposite row is now your partner. Please sit down."

Emerson and I have escaped the first round of cuts it seems.

"If you are left-handed, please move to the middle." Only three come forward this time. "Hmm … and if you have a widow's peak hairline, please go ahead and join the lefties." Again, Emerson and I stay where we are, while Dr. Albright pairs up all of those who are in the middle, like they are about to board a genetics Noah's Ark.

I silently count those who remain. There are twelve of us. Then two people with attached earlobes are grouped together.

"If you can roll your tongue, move to the middle," Dr. Albright calls out.

Finally, I have cause to move and so does Emerson, who neatly tucks a stray hair behind her ears, avoiding her glasses, as she moves forward. I've seen her do this gesture over a dozen times. I think she draws strength from it. I try doing the same, but my untamable hair just springs free to fall however it likes. I catch Emerson shaking her head at me. This girl never misses a thing, that is, except *me*.

A guy taps me on the shoulder, breaking my eye contact with Emerson. Grrr! I try not to appear angry when I turn to him. "Bro, am I doing it?" he asks, sticking a flat tongue out at me. I shake my head and the poor guy looks dejected but returns to the back row. Witnessing this, the rest of us in the middle curl and brandish our rolled tongues, double-checking one another's claim to be in the current grouping.

Emerson sticks her tongue out at me like a taunt, and I chuckle and return the childish gesture. I feel like I'm in kindergarten. But damn, seeing her curled, pink tongue looks hot, and I'm immediately picturing other things she can do with it.

"Do any of you tongue-rollers have dimples?" Dr. Albright asks. "If so, raise your hand."

I crack the biggest grin not only to show my left dimple, but because I fucking know Emerson has the cutest, little dimples when she smiles, although the stubborn brat is not lifting her arm. She knows what it means if she does, since it's just the two of us left with this trait it seems. I open my mouth to call her out on her evasion, but there is no need. Emerson quickly shoots her arm up in the air, all the while glaring at me. "Another match," calls out Dr. Albright. "Please take a seat."

Sit? I feel like stage diving.

Eventually, everyone is matched except one student, so Dr. Albright assigns him to a pair of pretty girls and announces that he can be part of a ménage, which gets a few laughs. His partners give him a high five when he joins them. There are no such congratulations from Emerson, who hasn't looked my way since sitting back down at our initial seats up front. Nope, she is scribbling circles in her notebook so intently, you'd think she was curing cancer.

"For your first assignment, you will need to list out each other's hereditary and acquired traits. Then, hypothesize what your children would look like based on dominant and recessive traits they might inherit. If you're in a same-sex group, one of you will have to fudge that part for science's sake. Instructions on how to do a probable genetic coin toss are in our online classroom page. Oh, and you'll need to know your blood type, so if you're not sure what it is, please head to the graduate clinic or the lab diagnostics center in town to schedule a blood draw ASAP. And now …," Dr. Albright says, dragging it out for dramatic effect, "here is something you probably never heard a teacher say before. 'Go forth and procreate!'"

Oh, yeah, I'm loving this class!

3

EMERSON

THERE IS no possible way I can drop the class. It would screw up all my course plans for next semester and senior year. I'm so consumed with tallying the credits I'd still need that I barely miss a soaring Frisbee to the head. I know better than to cut across the campus green on a sunny day, but I had to clear my mind and get as far away from the science department and Steel as possible.

But nope, it's not working. Like it or not, I'm once again stuck with Steel. And to be clear, I like it not. Why I need to clarify this point to my own self, I have no idea. This is how flustered and worked up he gets me.

How he's always flummoxed me from the very first day my father assigned me to show the new celeb transfer around Franklin. I'd done the same for dozens of students before him, but a guy like Steel didn't need my help adjusting to a new school. He'd made more friends by the end of his first day than I did after my entire time there.

I can hear footsteps behind me. "Emerson, wait up," Steel calls out, chasing after me. His long strides catch up to mine despite my attempt at speedwalking. "Don't you want my number?"

I spin around to face him, hands on my hips. He's not even out of breath, yet I feel my lungs constrict just looking at his ridiculously handsome face. "Oh, I have your number," I say, and I'm proud at how sassy it came out.

Steel does a double take, obviously confused. "You do?"

"Well, no, not really," I say, my bluster ebbing away. "I meant it figuratively, like, I have your number, Mister."

"Mister?" Steel laughs and even that sounds sexy. "I hope you're not planning on becoming a schoolteacher because that was the worst attempt at being stern ever. More like a cute bunny trying to stand up to a speeding car."

Hmph. I can be stern. I think. "Let me get this straight. You're calling *me* a bunny but comparing yourself to a car?" I murmur, smothering a smile.

He nods with that little smirk he always gave me. "An exotic sports car."

Like usual, he has the uncanny ability to make me want to swear and laugh at the same time. Glancing heavenward, I call for patience and come up with zilch. Pivoting on my foot, I turn to leave, but the grass sort of slumps inward here, forming a hollow, which is why everyone appropriately calls this area of the campus green "the pit." My ankle twists and I teeter. Horrified, I picture myself rolling down the incline and into the group of students sunbathing below.

Before I can scream, though, Steel reaches out to clasp my arms. Righting me, he hauls my backside up against his defined wall of a chest. It feels more intimate than it should with his chin practically resting in the crook of my neck, but not touching. My skin feels scorched with heat just the same and my stomach muscles tense in response to his touch. "I gotcha," Steel says, his warm breath tickling my ear, and I shudder. "You're okay," he soothes, mistaking my tremor for fear and not instinctual pleasure. Slowly, Steel releases his hold but continues to hover close as if ready to grab me again if necessary.

"Thank you," I mutter, glancing back down at the group below, lying out in their swim trunks and bikinis. It could have been much worse.

Although, this means yet another one of my blunders witnessed by Steel. He's known me since an awkward preteen, so he's seen my clumsiness plenty of times. I doubt I could list them all out if I wanted to. But who's counting?

Especially not when I have a more important question. "What are you doing here?" I ask, grasping the only thought circling my brain since laying eyes on Steel again.

With a chuckle, he lifts his palms up in an innocent 'who, me?' gesture. "I'm here to rescue you?"

I scowl at him, not returning his sensual smile. He knew very well what I meant.

"I take it back," he says, shifting his stance. "*That* is the look of one tough teacher."

"Why are you *here* at Thatcher College?" I repeat. "Where have you been the last two years?"

He places a warm hand gently on the small of my back and leads me toward the walking path, which I should have stayed on to begin with instead of taking the shortcut. Little good it did me.

"I'm here because Thatcher is a prestigious college, and it's as far away from the West Coast as I could get," he says with a shrug, echoing my own reasons for applying. I nod, urging him to continue. "As for the last couple of years, I managed my dad's European tour and took remote classes, working my ass off to get in here."

He must have because a 3.5 GPA is a Thatcher requirement, and Steel barely graduated from Franklin. I know this because my father lamented about Steel each night, regaling us over dinner with his latest prank, failure, you name it. I probably shouldn't know half of the things I know about Steel, but I suppose being the daughter of the dean comes with a few perks. Not many, but inside information on Steel was the main highlight.

Then again, he did shock everyone by scoring a 1450 on his first SAT test. So yeah, I know he's no dummy, he just acts like one. Not to mention his only extracurricular activity at Franklin was partying his ass off. All right, I suppose managing a global band would count as extra credit, especially if he applied to the business school, which is the most popular degree here. Or maybe his dad pulled some major strings, no guitar pun intended. I snort at my own joke. I'll have to use that another time.

But this is clearly not the time. Steel is looking at me oddly, and no wonder. I'm standing in the quad, laughing at my own unvoiced musings like an imbecile.

"The odds of you being here though," I grumble, unsure what else to say. "If roughly twenty thousand people apply, and only a total of nine hundred are accepted, that's about 4.5 percent. But then again, the number of transfers accepted is likely even lower, and that's not accounting for how many US colleges there are to choose from in the first place." I look up at Steel as if he'll have the probability solution for me, but all I get is a blank stare. Yup, I'm pretty sure I was better off remaining mute.

Steel shrugs, obviously not as astounded by this coincidence as I am. "Um … as I was saying, we should probably exchange numbers so we can coordinate for our group assignments," he reiterates, passing me his cell phone.

I nod, accepting his outstretched device, and tap in my contact info. His background screen is of an empty open-air music arena with the sun setting behind it. I don't know why, but it makes me feel sad.

"That was in Madrid," Steel says, as if reading my mind before pocketing his phone.

"It looks so forlorn, yet beautiful at the same time," I whisper.

Steel's gray eyes snap to mine and I stare back, locked in an unexpected moment, everything around us fading to the foreground. It's intense, and I'm not even sure why, but I feel a pull to him that eclipses anything I've ever felt before. For some unknown reason, I wish nothing more than to both comfort him *and* be comforted at the same time.

"That's exactly what I thought," Steel says huskily, his dark-gray eyes turning smokier. The pit of my stomach is doing summersaults, and I can feel goose bumps breaking out on my skin, but I no longer care if he notices it or not. "I sat alone on that stage long after the sun disappeared, unable to pull away."

Like me now.

Shaking my head, I try to rid myself of whatever spell has me in this Steel trance. "When do you want to meet?" I ask, clearing my suddenly hoarse throat.

"Uh …" Steel does a similar flinch, finally breaking his gaze and releasing his invisible hold on me.

"I'd like to get started on the first assignment before the weekend," I butt in, all business. *Nicely done, Em!*

Steel bobs his head in agreement. "Cool, me too. My dad's going to be playing in Boston this weekend, so I'm heading down there on Friday night. How about this Wednesday? My last class is at three."

"Great, so how about four then?" I ask, already putting the meeting in my phone's calendar.

"Great," Steel agrees, and I'm pretty sure he's repeating my exclamation to annoy me. "My dorm room?"

Yeah, I don't think so, buddy. "The library would be better," I state firmly.

Steel shrugs. "I'm living over in Youth—you know, the no-alcohol, quiet dorm—so it's ideal for studying in the future too."

"Ha, sure you are," I say, rolling my eyes. Steel in the substance-free dormitory? Yeah right, and Snoop Dog only smokes candy cigarettes.

"I am," Steel corrects me, sounding serious. "I'm no longer that guy from Franklin Academy, Em. I've been sober for two years now." Tugging his keychain holder out of his bag, he holds up some sort of metal medallion attached to it. A sobriety chip.

"Oh," I say, removing my thoughtless foot from my big mouth. "That's amazing, Steel. Good for you!"

He nods, smiling once again. "Yup, I'm a changed man," Steel says, shoving his hands into his snug jean pockets.

Seriously, wow! What kid our age has gone through the program already? It couldn't have been easy. I step forward, wanting to hug him encouragingly, but I stop myself just in the nick of time. He's not your friend. You barely know him. He's just a popular guy who, yet again, is going to the same school as you. And here you go, almost falling at his feet like one of his dad's fans. Don't you dare be another one of his groupies!

"We'll see," I respond, my hands on my hips. I have no idea why it came out sounding like a dare. This sassy chick in charge of my mouth today is not the usual tongue-tied me.

Steel smirks at me. That smirk does things to me. That smirk is highly problematic.

"We shall." He says this like it's a promise.

Grr.

"Did you just growl at me?" he asks, and I freeze, not realizing I'd made the noise out loud.

"Maybe," I admit, like it's no biggie.

Steel's lethal smile only grows, and I try not to gulp.

We shall indeed.

4

───────────

EMERSON

"Did you hear? Diesel's son is a junior here now. I wonder if we're going to see his dad on campus too."

The familiar gossip echoing around the library is triggering my Franklin Academy PTSD. I literally heard the same whispers when Steel transferred during sophomore year there too. I am trying my best to ignore it, but it's no use. Steel's name is on everyone's lips, or at least his father's is.

"Do you think Diesel will perform at our senior formal?"

Argh! I prop my textbook upright, forming a puny barrier wall in front of me. I've read the same paragraph on symbiosis three times so far, and the words aren't sinking in, only the murmurs of others.

"This is way cooler than the senator's daughter attending."

Who just so happens to be one of my friends, but whatever. I shake my head and go back to my failed attempts at reading.

"Well, if it isn't Belle with her nose stuck in a book,"

comes Steel's annoyingly familiar voice, and my book wall collapses with a thud. A guy seated at the table in front of me has the nerve to turn around and shush me —the same person who was just gossiping away about Steel. When he sees who I'm with, though, he smiles and gives Steel a manly nod. Typical.

"Huh?" I ask, looking up at Steel who's looming over the desk I reserved for us. He's in gym clothes, but even they look designer. Not grubby and loose like the ones I own. Not that I bother to go to the gym. They are more for lounging and contemplating working out.

"You know, from *Beauty and the Beast*," Steel says, sounding surprised that I failed his pop-culture quiz. "Although, she wasn't devouring a bio textbook."

I hear a feminine snort next to us and turn to find my friend April Harris standing there, observing us. "I got that reference," she says proudly while balancing about a dozen books in her arms, like always. Not textbooks, like my classes require, but a copy of *Les Miserables* and other English Literature works. "Sorry to interrupt," she adds, glancing between Steel and me.

"Hi, there, I'm Steel," he says, flashing the petite April a smile. "I'd shake your hand, but …" He motions toward the stack of books she's cradling, which equal almost half her height. "Would you like some help?" Steel offers, reaching out for her bookstack, but April quickly shakes her head, her sleek bob bouncing.

"No, I'm used to it. April."

"Excuse me?" Steel asks, his turn to look confused.

I don't blame him, considering it's currently the second week of September, but April likes to use her month-inspired name to mess with people. I've learned to stay clear of her on April Fools' Day, too, since she likes to pretend it's her own personal holiday. And while I'd like to think we both have a sharp wit, April is much better at spitting out her quips than I am. Mine seem to rattle around in my brain, spewing forth only after no one is around to hear them, which amounts to a heaping pile of woulda, shoulda, couldas.

"April is her name," I clarify. "She's majoring in English Lit here. We both live over in Tasker Hall, but she's on the first floor." And I'm clearly rambling.

"Ah," Steel says, slipping into the empty chair next to me. "Nice to meet ya."

"Likewise," April responds, but she is staring at me instead with a peculiar look. It's unnerving. Without any words uttered, I know she's silently asking why I'm hanging out with him.

"Um … Steel and I know each other from prep school," I rush out, not sure why I'm volunteering this information, but April has a way of doing that.

"Old friends," Steel supplies.

April's dark eyebrows shoot up, and I don't bother to correct Steel on the *friend* part while in front of her. We're not even *new* friends, never mind old ones.

"We've been assigned as lab partners this semester," I add under her scrutiny. Yup, April is going to be asking me a lot more questions later, but at least she isn't now. No, she's getting us to talk with unnerving stares and arched eyebrows alone, like a clever Ravenclaw wizard.

"Okay, *friends*, I'll leave you to it then," April says sweetly, but then she purses her lips, her thoughts suddenly elsewhere. She tends to drift away at random like that, as if she's reading a book in her head or something. "Hopefully, Cal left for his track meet and is no longer blaring me out of my dorm room like some wannabe DJ."

"Cal Chase?" Steel asks all smiles, and I'm not even surprised. But of course, he knows the other cool kids on campus already, even upper classmen.

"The one and only," April grumbles, shifting her bookstack for a better grip.

"Just met him earlier today," Steel shares. "Nice guy."

"It would be *nice*, if I didn't share a wall with him," April retorts. "Anywho, later, you two."

"That rhymes," Steel points out, and April is smiling again. "If you'd like for me to say anything to Cal about the volume of his music, just let me know."

"Nah, I can handle him," April responds, sounding overly confident, but I can't argue with her assessment. Although she may be tiny, so are pit bulls! Still, I have a feeling April wouldn't know what to do with Cal if she ever should *handle* him. Thou dost protest too much, if you ask me, but I'm keeping quiet on that front since I got my head chewed off the last time she complained about her handsome neighbor. But I still say there is more to their fighting than she lets on. Besides, Cal seems like a decent guy, especially for a senior and a star athlete on the track team. But he's April's problem. I have my own thorn in my side to deal with. I shoot Steel a glance and am shocked he's looking at me and not at my adorable friend.

"Bye, Wednesday," Steel says teasingly with a wave as April heads out.

"Ha! I've heard June, August, pretty much every month, but that was the first day of the week. Good one." April glides away gracefully, despite the load she carries, and I turn to find Steel's eyes smiling into mine once more. Yes, his eyes are smiling. I've heard people use that term before, but I've never been able to do it. *He* can, and my lips turn up in response. It's infectious.

"I like her," he says. "I can easily see you two being friends."

"I hope that's a compliment."

"Definitely," he says, powering up his laptop and placing it on the table in front of us.

Eager to get started too, I scoot my stuff to the side to make room. "Speaking of which, since when are we *friends?*" I ask, using air quotes on the *friends* portion of my question. "You never gave me the time of day at Franklin, and now that you're here at Thatcher, all of a sudden, we're besties?"

"*You* never gave ME the time of day," Steel says with an incredulous shake of his head.

He's trying to lay the blame on me? I roll my eyes, letting him know exactly what I think of him turning things around.

Steel only nods with a grin. "Good girls like you never do."

Good girl? Not loving that descriptor, even if it is accurate.

"It's true," he says emphatically. "I'd try talking to

you, but you'd assume the worst, as if I was trying to mess with you or something."

Because you were, I almost scream, but I bite my tongue, remembering how I'd sometimes catch him looking at me searchingly, like he was asking for my help somehow. No, that was just my wishful thinking. I shake my head to both clear my fanciful thoughts and to strengthen my resolve.

"Oh really? How about the time you prank-called me and asked me to prom?" I ask, pointing an accusatory finger at him. Just remembering it has me mortified all over again.

"Listen," he commands, shocking me by grabbing my pointed finger and enclosing his fist gently around it. An electric current runs up my arm from his warm touch, making me squirm in my seat. Looking deeply into my eyes, he adds, "That wasn't a prank."

"Oh, I see. So not only am I a good girl, but I'm gullible too?" I pull my hand back and bring it to rest on my lap. "I heard your friends laughing in the background."

"They were laughing because you flat-out said no," he states, sounding dead serious.

But that's crazy. Steel would never have really asked me out, which is why I didn't even go to my senior prom. I didn't want to see him and his group of entitled, rich friends laughing at me when I entered alone, and my dad chaperoning. But … I think back to his phone call, and I'm no longer sure if it was malicious after all. Steel doesn't leave me time to ponder further though.

"So, *partner*," Steel says, sounding cheerful again and

gesturing to his computer screen as if nothing else had been discussed. "I already started the genetics questionnaire and filled out the obvious stuff like, dimples, hair color, eye color, etc."

I'm amazed by his initiative and the fact that he knew so many of my traits without having me near to double-check. I scan over what he's inputted, and sure enough, it's all correct. He even guessed my height at five foot seven. Although technically, I'm five foot six and three quarters, but I usually round it up too. Steel's column lists his height as five foot eleven, which seems conservative since I always assumed he was at least six feet tall, if not more. My perusal comes to an immediate stop when I see that he's listed his eye color as dark brown.

"You have gray eyes," I point out, baffled. How can he think otherwise?

"I do?" he asks, arching an eyebrow as if this is news to him.

"Yeah, they are steel colored, like your name. Isn't that why you were named Steely?"

"No," he says, shaking his head with a laugh, his black, silky bangs falling over one steel-colored eye. It takes all of my concentration not to sigh and move the locks out of his way. "My dad named me after the musician Steely Dan, and my middle name, Nash, is for both the city of Nashville and the group Crosby, Stills & Nash."

Interesting. "Hmm … well, I guess when you have a dad who goes by Diesel, your kid needs a badass name too."

Steel's grin tugs up at the corner. "You think my name is badass?"

I roll my eyes. "You know it is."

He shrugs. "I guess I can't complain since I was almost named Clapton Hendrix. Imagine, Hey Clap! Sounds like an STD."

I giggle at his horrified expression. "Or Cobain Van Halen. That would be a mouthful," I say.

Now Steel chuckles, and it fills me with pleasure. "I guess we can't all be named after poets like Ralph Waldo Emerson," Steel says, leaning in to nudge me lightly with his shoulder.

I suck in a shocked breath. "How did you know that?"

"You mentioned it in the essay you wrote for our Creative Writing class. The teacher had you read it aloud."

I nod, remembering it, but am surprised Steel paid any attention to something I was reading. "Yes, well, either way, there is no way your eyes are run-of-the-mill brown."

Steel is quiet for a second, as if taking this in. "Well, either way," he mimics, "nothing compares to your brilliant-blue orbs." He then clears his throat. "Sad to say, the probability of our children also having blue eyes is only 25 percent. But I'm hoping at least one will be lucky enough to inherit your superpower of striking men brainless with a mere cobalt look."

"Children?" I squeak out, not sure which part of his shocking remark to focus on. I've overheard Steel's charm in effect before but never had his bullshit aimed at me.

"Oh yeah, we'd need a few. I figure since we're both an only child, it would be nice to have a great big family."

"Yes," I say a little too wistfully. "I've always wanted three."

"Then you got it, sweetheart," he says, waggling his eyebrows, and my heartbeat accelerates.

"Not with you!" I'm quick to rectify. Is it my imagination, though, or did Steel's face fall at my rejection? His expression shifted too fast for me to be sure, and now his usual smug grin is in place.

"Tell that to Dr. Albright because for our first assignment, we are two chromosome babymakers theorizing what DNA we'll share with the next generation," he says, reminding me of what we're really talking about. Right. Duh. He wasn't really thinking about having babies with me. I want to laugh at my own stupidity for even imagining it for the briefest of seconds. "From what I'm seeing in this probability chart," Steel says, leaning closer to me, "our kids are going to be smart and gorgeous, just like their mama." He winks one steely eye.

I stiffen in my seat. All right, enough of this false charm. Steel being himself is a force to be reckoned with, but when he turns up the charisma, it's freakin' overwhelming, especially to a thirsty girl like me. I shove him with my elbow and he chuckles, returning to his side where he belongs. The distance doesn't stop my pulse from racing any less though.

"You can't argue that they'd already have a built-in name for their band—Steely Powers."

"Or Powers of Steel," I say, putting my last name first. Okay, so I may or may not have doodled our names together like that and in several other combinations before. I stifle a sigh, picturing my ole naive self, almost wishing I could go back and slap her and tell her to snap out of it. But here I am again, imagining not just our names together, but our bodies.

"I like it," he agrees with a wink. "Or Nash Powers? Nah, sounds too much like a detective show."

I laugh again, not sure if I've ever felt so comfortable with a guy before, never mind Steel. Averting my gaze, I look back to the questionnaire and spot a blank row for where our blood types should go. "I'm A+, just like my grades," I say, tapping at the screen and repeating the same lame joke I've said a dozen times since finding out my blood type as a kid.

Steel humors me, at least with a smile. "I wanna say I'm B positive, like my attitude, but I have no idea. Not to worry though," he says, pulling back the sleeve of his sweater, revealing a black guitar pick tattoo on the inner side of his wrist and a fresh Band-Aid in the crook of his arm. "I just got back from the clinic. I should have a full workup before the weekend."

"Perfect," I say, not bothering to mask how impressed I am that he didn't wait till the last minute. So far, I couldn't have asked for a better partner to be paired with. I just didn't expect it to be Steel. Not in a million years.

We continue filling out the remaining columns, run

probability rates for our theoretical spawn, and are almost done, except for his blood type.

"It's funny," he says, looking philosophical. "I know that my dad's is AB and my mom was A negative, but I never thought to check mine."

"Hmm." I flip back a page in our textbook to the blood type and Rh compatibility predictor charts. "That means, you'll be some sort of A or B variation too. But I'm curious, how do you know theirs and not yours?"

"I remember Sheila's from her autopsy report, and I guess it stuck with me." He says this so matter-of-factly that it almost breezes over how truly terrible his statement is. My heart constricts with pain for both him and his mother, Sheila, who, from what I've heard, had her share of demons and addictions.

"I'm sorry," I say automatically, frowning deeper, knowing that my comment sounds so useless and not nearly enough, but I'm also not sure what else to say.

His mouth in a grim line, Steel barely nods. "And while managing Diesel's tour, some of the foreign stadiums required extra health requirements, like hiring a private ambulance or having a defibrillator, EpiPen, as well as extra blood on hand." He shakes his head with a lopsided grin. "Rockers don't have the best reputations for being safe bets."

"Wow, that sounds like a lot to manage." I'm already imagining all the color-coded lists I'd have to write, if I were in his shoes, just to keep everything organized.

Steel shrugs like it's no big deal. "It was pretty much the same process after I did it once, but handling transportation for everyone, on the other hand, or security and visas … those were a bigger bitch to manage than the insurance requirements."

"I bet," I say, even more impressed. I figured lots of behind-the-scenes details went into putting on a concert, but those particulars hadn't occurred to me.

"Speaking of tours," Steel says, "I can hook you up with backstage passes to this weekend's show if you'd like."

Something about Steel's halfhearted smirk and offer doesn't feel right. I'm not saying that he doesn't genuinely mean it—he seems sincere enough—but his voice took on a jaded edge. I've never asked him for tickets before, even though most of Franklin went to at least one Diesel show as a VIP at some point.

I shake my head. "No thanks." Besides, I'd have no way of paying him back for the tickets and nothing to offer in exchange.

"It's no problem. I'll leave your name at the box office. Wait, what?" His head jolts back as if I'd just slapped him.

"I'm good," I answer, not sure why he is looking at me like I have two heads.

"Seriously?"

My brow furrows. "Yeah. What's the big deal? You sound almost irritated that I'm not jumping up and down at the chance at a backstage pass."

"Not irritated," he says, slowly shaking his head. "Mystified."

I shrug. "No offense, but I'm not a fan of your dad's music."

"No offense, but I was not a fan of *your* dad's

attendance policy," Steel throws back, jokingly mocking my voice. "Also saying 'no offense' at the start of a sentence doesn't make it any less offensive."

I open and close my mouth. "You're right. I hate when people say that or 'just kidding,' and here I just did. Sorry." Steel nods in forgiveness, and I scramble to dig myself, once again, out of a Steel-induced hole of embarrassment. I don't know what my deal is lately, as I usually never say half the stuff I'm thinking, yet around Steel, I'm a sieve. "Your dad's music is, of course, great. Everyone knows it. It's just that alternative rock isn't my jam."

"And what *is* your jam?" he asks playfully, his eyes warm again.

I don't hesitate. "Raspberry jam … with a warm, chocolate croissant from Starbucks."

Steel laughs for real, and the happy sound draws the looks of the students around us, who I'll admit I forgot were even here this last hour working together. Like I've been in a Steel bubble that's now popped.

"You're such a goofball, it's endearing," he says sweetly and inside I melt.

While it's hardly a glowing compliment, I'm flattered just the same, overly pleased that he gets my goofiness. I'm especially proud that I've managed, in the last five minutes, to both shock him and get a real laugh, not one of his cynical ones. Why I care about either of these accomplishments, I have no idea. Old habits, or rather crushes, die hard, I guess.

"I—I enjoyed his recent love song though. I know it wasn't a big hit, but I'm a sucker for lyrics, and for once,

I was able to understand them," I admit, chuckling to myself for being the dork he just called me and not a rock fan like most people.

"You liked the lyrics in that song?" Steel asks, oddly serious once again.

"Yes, they're beautiful." Closing my eyes for a moment, I recall and then recite my favorite part: *"She turned her tender eyes to me. As deep as any ocean. As sweet as any harmony."*

When I open them, Steel is gaping and looking at me like … well, I don't know what. Crap! Was it weird that I just quoted his dad's song to him? I know we're in a library, but suddenly, I can't take the silence—Steel's silence!

He shakes his head. "I wrote that."

"Ha! Sure you did."

"I did! Google it!" he says, his cool-guy mask returning.

"I will."

"Good."

"Good." Yes, I can hear that I sound like a child, and I take a deep breath in an attempt to regain my maturity. "Seriously? You wrote that?" Steel nods, and without having to fact-check it, I believe him. "It's poetry, Steel. You have a gift."

He waves off my compliment with a bat of his hand. "Thanks, Emerson, but as you know, it's not rocket science. That I'll leave up to geniuses like you."

I flinch and begin packing up my stuff. "I'm no genius, I just work hard," I spit back defensively. It's the same kind of mocking I used to hear at Franklin, the kind of comments I thought I'd left behind three thousand miles away. "We're done here."

"Whoa, Emerson," Steel says, placing a hand on my shoulder, stopping me from rising as I was planning on doing. "I meant it as a good thing, not an insult."

I shrug his hand off and get to my feet. "Have fun in Boston," I call out, not bothering to face him again. "I'll see you in class on Monday."

Naturally, my grand exit is marred by sideswiping my hip against one of the desks as I race out of there. Ouch! Better my hip than Steel continuing to bruise my ego.

5

EMERSON

Boom! Boom!

Pissed off, I pound on Steel's door with my fist, loud enough to disturb everyone in Youth dormitory. But my last text to him still shows as unread, so I've been left with no choice but to track him down in person.

And here I was beginning to think being partnered up with Steel wasn't going to be so bad after all. Wrong! I mean, who ditches the first official lecture? Especially after Dr. Albright plainly said there would be a quiz on it accounting for half of our grades. And if he fails, I fail!

I'm going to kill him. He might not be taking college seriously, but I must, or my scholarship will be revoked.

"Steel!" I yell from the hallway, raising my fist to bang on the wooden door once more, but he opens it before I can make contact, causing me to stumble forward, colliding with his chest. Again! This time, it's my front mashed up against him. My nose smacking into a brick wall of muscle.

"Ouch," I mutter and shove away.

I look up, expecting to find Steel laughing at my usual clumsiness, but he's already turned and walking back into his room. His very dark room. The shades are drawn, and the lights are off. It's after noon. Was his lazy ass still sleeping? Without asking, I step inside, the door automatically closing behind me. Brushing my hands against the wall, I locate the light switch and punch it on a little too forcefully, still trying to diffuse my anger. Once my eyes adjust to the overhead fluorescent lighting, I locate Steel, who is sitting, slouched on his twin bed, his face buried in his hands and his propped elbows resting on his legs. To make things even more solemn, he's wearing a black hoodie drawn over his head, further obscuring his face.

Belatedly realizing something isn't right here, my hostility deflates faster than a pricked balloon. "Steel?" I ask, cautiously crossing the room to stand near him. "Are you okay?"

"No."

Alrighty … I'm not sure what to make of his one-word response, but given how raw he sounded, I know that whatever the problem is, it's serious.

"Are you sick?"

"No." This time, he at least does a headshake too.

Feeling useless, I continue to stand here with no clue what to say next. My hand reaches out to him on its own accord, but I draw it back, not sure if he'll accept my comfort. "Did … um … did you fall off the wagon?"

He scoffs. "No."

"No," I repeat. Exasperated and unsure what to do now, I sit down next to him on his unmade bed. My added weight to the mattress causes Steel to sway slightly toward me, and when his arm brushes against mine, he doesn't scoot away and neither do I. A moment or two pass in silence, then he leans more against my side. Okay, I'm totally freaked. Something is majorly wrong.

As gently and as encouragingly as I can manage, I ask, "What is it, Steel?"

"My blood type is O," he says hoarsely, finally turning to face me. I gasp, seeing his face so pale and awash in pain. Dark circles are showing under his sharp gray eyes. And despite all this he's still so handsome. This time, I don't stop my hand from reaching out to rest on his arm.

"I wasn't asking about that. Our lab report isn't due till the end of the week," I sputter, reassuringly rubbing my hand up and down his arm. "I—I want to know what's the matter."

Steel laughs soundlessly, and I can feel the movement against my roaming hand.

"The matter *is* my blood type. It's O."

"So?" I ask, feeling clueless, an emotion I don't care for at all. Steel looks at me expectantly, and I scramble to solve the problem he clearly thinks I know the answer to. And then … I do. "Oooo."

"Yup, O!"

Holy shit! There is no way a father with the blood type A could make an O child if his mate wasn't an O.

My mind is blown, so I can't even imagine how jumbled Steel's is given this news. "Uh … did you talk to your dad about it?"

"You mean the dad who isn't my dad?" he asks sarcastically. "Yeah. I got the results back from the lab while he was playing onstage, so there was no hiding my face when he entered his dressing room afterward."

Yikes! "How did he take it?"

"He already knew!" Steel exclaims, standing up to pace before me. "That was the real shocker, not my mom being with someone else. Those rumors I'd already heard plenty of over the years. But … but he's known since I was two. Back when he'd been fighting for full custody, and a paternity test revealed I wasn't his."

I try to process all this, and for the first time, I wish I'd bothered to watch those Maury Povich "you're not the father" video clips that people like to post. Then maybe I'd know what to say here. Maybe. "All right," I say, thinking aloud. "So, that means he knew but still chose to be your dad, to raise you, to love you, to give you his name and everything else. I'd say that makes him your real dad no matter what his blood type."

Steel stops his pacing, his posture sagging. He looks so tormented that I feel knots twisting in my own stomach for him. "I know, and he said pretty much the same thing when I confronted him," Steel says with anguish. Turning his head away from me for a second, he roughly wipes at his eyes. The covert motion is so quick, I almost miss it. As if I'd judge him if a tear rolled out. Hell, I'd be a bawling mess if the situation was reversed. "But … he should have told me." This comes out almost as a whisper, like he didn't mean to let the admission escape.

"Of course," I agree automatically, although I don't think my own parents would have told me either. They aren't the most communicative, at least not when it comes to feelings and stuff like this. It would be just another life lesson to shield me from and not deal with together. "I'm sure he was only trying to protect you," I reason.

Steel grunts and sits back down on the bed next to me, our bodies touching once again. "I realize that, but it doesn't make it any easier."

"No, of course not. This isn't easy at all."

"You know, it's ironic. Throughout my teenage years, I resented being Diesel's son, even did all I could to lash out at him for being in the spotlight. And now that I know I'm not his son, I just want to go back to before I knew," Steel says, emitting a self-loathing laugh. "I also want to punch my teenage self for even complaining about being his kid."

I purse my lips, considering what he just said. "Don't say that! Do you know how much I hated being the dean's daughter and how I wished my dad had any other career but that one? Doesn't mean I wanted a different father or anything. All kids go through stuff like that, it's normal."

"Normal," Steel repeats with a snort. "That's all I wanted. I would have given anything to have stable parents like yours, but now …" He trails off, looking heartbreakingly lost and vulnerable. "I just want my dad." My heart tightens in response. I wish I could take away his pain and throw my arms around him. Fuck it, I will.

I tug his hood down, and he turns his hurt, clouded eyes on me. Before I can stop myself, I'm pulling him closer for a hug. I'm surprised by the ferocity with which his arms wrap around me, drawing me closer in his embrace. He's taking slow, deep breaths, as if trying to calm himself, and I rise and fall with his inhales and exhales, holding him.

"It's all right," I croon to him, not sure if he's listening. Moving my hands to his shoulders, I give him a little squeeze. "You're doing okay though. Look at you. You're at an elite college, you're sober, and you managed an international tour, for fuck's sake. You're still badass, Steel. Diesel's son, no matter what."

Steel stares at me for a long moment, the dullness in his eyes that I saw earlier clearing. "You've never looked at me like that before," he says, his voice gravelly.

"Like what?"

"Like you finally see me," he states, and my stomach flips, afraid that he's seeing me, too, and how much I care about him. I take my own slow, deep breath, needing air, space, something to fill the emptiness I'm currently experiencing.

"What do you mean?" I ask, sounding way more blasé than I feel. Steel opens his mouth to answer, and my gaze focuses on his parted lips. God, how I want to suck on that bottom, lush lip of his. I feel tingly and hot all over. Steel smiles for the first time since I entered his room. Not just with his mouth, but with his eyes. Very gray eyes. I'm surprised to see interest there. Heat, too.

A shocked gasp lodges in my throat when I realize Steel is leaning in, and the mouth I was just staring at is coming closer. Yes!

He tastes my lips, capturing my mouth with a fierce kiss. Cupping my face, he holds me closer, tilting my head up toward his for better access. And I give it, exploring every inch of his mouth with mine. I bite his bottom lip like I've been dying to do for years, and then soothe the sting over with my tongue. A hungry growl vibrates in his throat, and I shiver with pleasure. Kissing Steel is more than I ever imagined, and I've done plenty of that. It's better! We're savoring each other like our lives and our very next breath depend on it.

"Jesus," Steel whispers against my mouth, rubbing his lips over mine. I tremble as his hands stroke the small of my back, tracing my spine and sending further sparks of desire throughout my body. I know we were just hugging before, but this is so different. It's not comforting, it's electric and … and shouldn't be happening!

I take advantage of the pause and push away from his heaving chest, creating some much-needed distance between me and the same sexy wall I had just clung to a second ago. The haze of lust is slowly clearing, and I realize I'm straddling his lap. When the hell did that happen? I jump up like I'm on fire, which figuratively I am. It's now my turn to pace as I look for my bag.

I might have fantasized about Steel for years, but I was never dumb enough to think it would amount to anything. How could it possibly work? He'll break my heart and move on to the next girl, like skipping to another song on an album. Even if I would love to, I'll just have to accomplish number seven with someone else, someone safer. Someone I don't have to work with.

"I'm sorry," Steel groans out, immediately coming to his feet too. He places a strong hand on my arm, stopping my panicked strides. "I didn't mean to kiss you."

So, you didn't mean to give me the best fucking kiss of my life and rattle my soul? Gee, thanks. "It's fine," I say, shrugging off his touch, but when I look back into his tormented eyes, I'm reminded of his earth-shattering news. "You're stressed out and upset, not thinking straight. I get it."

"No, that's not what I meant." Steel tries to explain, stepping in front of me and preventing my progress to the door, which I'm eyeing like the emergency cord I desperately need to pull to eject myself out of here pronto. "I'm not sorry about kissing you, I just didn't mean for it to happen like this. Please don't be mad."

Mad? I grab the backpack I'd dropped earlier, and for a second, I imagine swinging the heavy mass at his dumb head.

"Whatever, it was nothing," I say coldly, and he flinches as if I did hit him with my bag after all.

"Come on," he urges. "You're my only friend on campus."

Again with the *friends* term? After a kiss like that? This is exactly why I can't be friends with a guy like Steel, even if it comes with benefits like his sublime kisses. I'm not experienced enough to handle this, to handle *him*. We're total opposites, from different worlds.

I need to think, and to do so, I have to get away from Steel.

I reach for the door to leave, then remember why I barged into Steel's dorm room to begin with. Slipping my hand inside my bag, I grasp my notebook. "Here," I say, all business. "Do us both a favor and read over my notes from today's class since there might be a quiz."

Steel shoves his hands into the kangaroo pocket of his hoodie, not taking the notebook that I'm holding out to him. "Don't you need them?"

I shake my head. "I should be good. You take it," I insist, and he finally does.

"Thanks," he mumbles, and I continue to stand there for another moment.

It's the weirdest thing. I'm desperate to leave his presence, but at the same time, I don't want to. I also don't want our conversation to end like this. He was hurting, I was trying to comfort him, and emotions took over. A physical chain reaction, I guess. Plus, we need to work together for the next fifteen weeks, so build a bridge and get over it already, Emerson!

"Fine," I say to both myself and to him. "We're friends and I'm not mad."

Steel's wolfish smile, though, has me already questioning my declaration and sanity. And this is after just one kiss? Further proof that I'm way out of my league.

6

STEEL

As I ENTER THE CLASSROOM, I drink in the sight of Emerson casually dressed, her gorgeous, rich, brown hair cascading down her back. I envy anyone who gets to sit behind her and look their fill. Although, being seated next to her is just as rewarding and I gladly slip into my seat, even if it is way up in the front.

There is already a pop quiz resting on the hard desktop, which explains why Emerson is hunched over a paper, her pen racing to keep up with her answers. I reviewed her comprehensive, color-coded notes, so I'm prepared. I finish up only a moment or two after her, placing my test down on the teacher's desk in unison with Em. She shoots me an annoyed look, and it only makes me smile. Man, I seem to rile her without any effort on my part, and odder still, I'm into it. That must make me a glutton for punishment, or a sadist, or some psychobabble shit like that.

I also know I shouldn't have kissed her so soon. I

mean, I've been dying to, but me gutted open for her to see wasn't the time. It was just that she was so close and smelled so good. And when she looked up at me with such warmth in her blue eyes and threw her arms around me, well, damn, I couldn't help myself. Even if the timing wasn't right, our world-rocking kiss has been on my mind ever since, thankfully distracting me from the mess with my da—Diesel.

But can a sweet girl like her ever care for a messed-up guy like me? That's what I need to find out, which is why my great Emerson plan was to be friends first. Show her how I've changed, then and only then, maybe try to take things out of the friend zone. If she even wants to. I've told myself I'd settle for friendship, but just maybe, there could be more. After that kiss, I fucking want more, that's for certain, but first, I'm going to help her out. That's my new game plan, and I don't care what I have to do to get her to listen, but it's happening. And damn, it's going to be fun.

I shoot Emerson a wicked grin. Turning her head, she scrunches her nose and narrows her eyes before returning them back to Dr. Albright's slides being projected up on the screens in front of us. It's fucking adorable when she wrinkles her nose like that, and I have to stop myself from whistling with satisfaction. Especially when she sends me little looks under her lashes every now and then.

Since I'm still in possession of her beloved notebook, Emerson is taking down today's notes on loose-leaf paper with a shimmery, green pen. So, I open her notebook and jot down the key takeaways on a blank page. They might not be color-coded by topic like hers were, but I make sure they are detailed, hoping to impress her, at least when she reviews them.

After the lecture, we exit the classroom side by side like companionable friends would, and it feels natural.

"How are you doing?" she asks, lowering her voice so others don't hear.

"Better," I tell her, hoping to convince myself too. You're fine, Steel. Nothing has really changed. It just feels like it has. You just have no idea of your parentage or identity anymore, but whatever. No biggie.

Emerson nods and thankfully changes the subject. "How do you think you did on the test?"

"Aced it, thanks to your notes. Your color-coded lists were helpful," I say, handing her back the notebook. She is beaming with pride, and I almost hate to reveal what I'm about to say, but then again, eager as hell too. "But the list at the back of your book … now that was especially interesting."

Emerson halts, and I have to take a step backward to rejoin her. She's already flipping to the back of her notebook, searching for her "Up to No Good" list. I mean, who names a list that? Who even makes a list of such things? This girl. This unique girl. I try to tamper down my grin, but I can't. Her list has given me such insight into the walled-up Emerson, not to mention an opportunity too.

"You can cross off number six since we already hooked up," I say, pointing to the scribbled item, but she slaps my hand away like a buzzing mosquito and whips her head around to see if anyone overheard me. No one else is left in the hallway though. Besides, would that be so bad? If people knew we made out? Her horrified reaction riles me more than I expected.

"That wasn't hooking up," she states, lifting a noble chin and pushing her glasses up her nose with her index finger. Why such a brush-off would be a turn-on is beyond me, but dammit, it is.

"If you don't consider sitting on my lap and making out 'hooking up,' then I'd love for you to demonstrate what *your* definition is. Please, I'm all ears, or rather, hands and lips."

Her eye roll is so big, I'm surprised her irises aren't stuck that way, like parents in movies warn kids about.

"Congratulations! You now have more embarrassing fodder to hold over me, is that it?"

I shake my head. "No, I just want to help."

"Ha!" She huffs and tromps out of the science wing, forcing me to follow in her wake.

"I mean it, Emerson!" I say, tugging on her arm so she'll stop and look at me and see that I'm serious, all teasing aside. "I'm not making fun of you, I promise. You want to have some fun at college, and you deserve that." I'm taking it as a good sign that she's not hitting me with her notebook or running away, so I press my point. "And who better to help you? Spoiler—it's me, obviously."

Emerson plops down on a nearby wooden bench under an old oak tree, and I'm relived I won't have to chase her across the green for a second time. Carefully, like I'm approaching a feral cat, I sit down beside her, ready to spring if attacked. She's not hissing, at least.

Clearing my throat, I try again. "Only look at number two on your list, and you'll see I'm your man. How many pranks did I pull at Franklin?"

"Well, just to name a few," she says with a purposeful look, clearly gearing up the evidence against me. "There was the time you hired a look-alike to go to school in your place while you went on a ski trip to Mammoth, but then stupidly posted photos to your stories from the mountain. Or the time you filled the film studies classroom with popcorn and released hundreds of bouncy balls in the cafeteria to ricochet off the walls and surfaces. Oh, and the time you managed to stream elevator music through the announcement speakers. Playing Diesel would have been too obvious, but really, who else could it have been? None of the privileged douches in your inner circle were smart enough to pull something like that off."

"So, you think I'm smart?" I ask, but she's on a roll and is either ignoring me or not listening.

"And of course, there was the time you and your crew locked me in the closet before my valedictorian speech."

My wince is real, and the incident flashes through my brain like I'm airing an episode of someone else's life —one that I never want to see again. It's the moment that changed everything for me.

"I'm so sorry, Emerson, really," I say as earnestly as possible, hoping she will believe me, but actions speak louder than words, and I know Emerson is the type who needs proof. "I swear on my mother's grave I had no idea they were planning to do that, but Joshua was pissed at your father for holding him back another year, so the spoiled jerk took it out on you. It's no excuse, and believe me, I'll never forget when I finally got the door open and your tender eyes turned to me. God, the look you gave me … well, fuck, it gutted me."

"Th-then," she trembles out, continuing the memory. Seeing the hurt clouding her eyes as she recalls the next part has me cringing anew. "Joshua suggested you all should see what I was hiding under my graduation robes. Before I could pull away, you shoved me toward the door and swung around and punched him in the nose." I can still hear the crunching sound from the break, but I'd do it again to keep her safe. "Oh, God, but when the blood started gushing out like a geyser, I took off just as they were calling me up on stage. My voice shook at first, but everyone assumed it was nerves, and not because of assholes like you."

I don't bother to defend myself or lay the blame on Joshua. I should have paid more attention to their whisperings. I should have chosen better friends. The fucker even sued my dad for damages. Money well spent. But it's the last part of what she says that I need to convince her is no longer true.

"I'm an asshole?"

"If you hang around with assholes," she says, like the end conclusion is obvious.

"Good to know," I state, trying to keep my temper in check and my disappointment hidden. "You were friends with the biggest airhead at Franklin. Does that make you one too?"

She frowns. "One, Heather has a good heart. Two,

how do you know who I was friends with? Three, point taken."

"You really *do* like lists," I say, trying to inject humor back into our conversation. But really, I'm marveling at how she's always quick to see reason, yet at the same time, so unperceptive about people, particularly me. Just another Emerson mystery. "Let me try it. One, I can't excuse my old crew or say their hearts are any good. When I stopped hooking them up with tickets and drugs … well, they left me quicker than my mom did outside the roadie trailer. Two, I know who you hung out with because I liked watching you, still do. Three, can we please start over? I'm not a bad guy, at least not anymore."

Sucking in her bottom lip, Emerson takes a moment to process what I just said, which is distracting AF. But while she stares past me at the cornhole match going on in the distance, I take advantage of the silence and continue, too afraid she'll reject what I'm saying before I have a chance to get it all out there.

"Speaking of lists, part of the twelve-step program is admitting our wrongdoings and listing anyone we might have harmed. I swear that I wasn't behind that stunt. Being friends with those assholes is my only wrongdoing when it comes to you, and for that, I'd like to make amends. I *need* to."

After what feels like an eternity, Emerson shakes her head, and my insides tighten as if bracing for her rejection.

"You don't play fair," she whines.

"How so?"

She takes a deep, restorative breath. "After the mom part and claiming I'm part of your recovery process, I can't very well say no to a do-over without being an asshole too."

See what I mean? I don't deserve her forgiveness but let it wash over me all the same, healing the emptiness inside and filling it with hope. My smile is huge, and it's all I can do not to lay a thousand grateful kisses over her beautiful face. But that I'll save for another day. I hope. Because speaking of lists, she checks off every box on mine.

Emerson lets out a small laugh. "Plus, whoever rebuilt Josh's nose made his face look even more weaselly, so thank you for that."

"Don't mention it," I say, laughing too. "So, can I please help you with your list?"

7

EMERSON

Am I seriously considering this?

Yes.

No.

Yes.

No way! Shaking my head, I stand to leave, but Steel calls out to me, and for whatever reason, I feel compelled to stop and hear him out.

"The other day, when you said I was on the right track," Steel says and I nod. "You're the reason why. After that incident at graduation, I took a step back and reevaluated everything. Because of *you*."

I turn around and point a finger at my chest. "Because of me?"

"Yes," Steel says, still sitting slouched on the bench and bobbing his head. "I didn't like the person I saw reflected in your eyes, and from that moment forward, I haven't been that guy. Now will you let me help you in return?"

He looks so sincere staring up at me, but I'm not used to trusting him or anyone else. I narrow my eyes with suspicion. "What's in it for you?"

He rubs his face. "Besides helping to corrupt the good girl?" he asks, laughing. I remain silent, refusing to fall for his charm, even if the idea of him *corrupting* me sends electricity to the pit of my belly. "It's as I said—a clean slate, making amends, and ... I think it will be fun."

"Fine. You can help me with the prank part," I concede, but he's shaking his head.

"I can help with more than just that," he says with a cocky grin as he rises to stand next to me.

I gulp. Does he mean helping in terms of my vCard? No, he couldn't be suggesting that. Despite this braver me, I don't dare touch that point on my stupid list. I can't believe I'm even agreeing to let him help me or that I haven't somehow dissolved in embarrassment at him reading my list in the first place. As much bravado as I can muster, I shove my mortification aside.

"You're new here. How can *you* help me secure an invite to a Greek party?" I look him up and down. "You're not even the frat-guy type." I leave out the fact that he's likely the type of many sorority girls though. Any girl for that matter.

"Thank you for noticing," he says proudly with an awe-shucks shrug. "Shouldn't be hard. I'll hand out some of Diesel's merch, suggest one day my dad will be dropping by to see me, and voila! I'm everyone's new best friend."

His cynical smile doesn't quite meet his eyes, and

once again, he catches me off guard with another one of his admissions. "That must suck," I say, picturing the scenario he's probably lived out dozens of times.

"Getting everything I want?" he asks sardonically while we companionably set off down the path toward the upper campus.

I glance over at him and then around. I feel like everyone is turning to watch us, or rather, him. Another downside to being a celebrity's kid, but one he must be used to by now. I know I've done my share of staring at Steel over the years too. "Yes. Thinking you have to buy your friends and not knowing if they are truly there because of who you are or for what you can get them."

His body stiffens. "Well, my dear, you just summed up my life in a nutshell. That expression is so weird, by the way," he says, deflecting, but oddly enough, I've also thought that before too. I fear I might be too literal for expressions like that because I never use them, and when I do, I'll often say them backward. "So," Steel says, "a Greek party, no problem. Clubbing? Got you covered there too. With my venue connections, I can get us into any club in town in just about any city you want."

"Us?" I ask, stopping.

"It's kind of a package deal," he says.

I nod and start walking again. It makes sense, as I suppose he'll need to be there for those scenarios.

"As for losing your virginity," he whispers, but I gasp as if he's just shouted it across the pit.

This is where I draw the line. "I'm not a charity case!"

"Believe me, it wouldn't be charity," he says huskily, and I huff out a breath not buying it, and his smile only deepens. "We'll pin that one for later because you were right to put it last on your list anyway. That is one experience you shouldn't rush into."

"Rush? I'm a twenty-year-old virgin. I'm hardly in the fast lane."

My admission brings out a bigger smile from Steel. I can't recall him ever being such a smiley type of guy, but since being at Thatcher, he's all smiles around me.

"Believe me, it makes a difference," he says soberly. "Especially if it's your first time."

"Whatever," I say testily because he sounds like my mother, and no one was asking for his opinion anyway. "I do *not* need your help with the rest of the stuff on my list." Liar! Simply imagining number seven with Steel has me flushing with heat. I shouldn't be feeling this hot in autumn in Maine! "I guess I can cross off number one on my list too."

Steel purses his so-kissable lips, trying to recall what I first put down. "Do something stupid?" he asks.

"Yes! Because agreeing to your help must be the stupidest thing I could ever do."

Instead of being insulted, Steel laughs. "Why don't you hold off on that one too. At least give me a shot to prove myself." He holds up his hands in a helpless gesture, but I'm still skeptical despite his innocent expression. Without waiting for me to agree, he continues. "We'll start with the ultimate prank."

"Not a mean one." I remind him of what I wrote in parenthesis.

"Of course. And just to clarify, all my pranks at Franklin were harmless too."

I can't argue, not now that I know he wasn't behind the graduation episode, and apparently, his asking me to prom was genuine, too, which is still blowing my mind. "All right, Prank Master, what do you have in mind?"

"I have a lot in mind," Steel mumbles cryptically. Hamming it up, he strokes his chin, appearing deep in thought. "But I think we should play upon your skills."

"*My* skills? What do you mean?"

"We're going to use science."

With the way my heart is racing, you'd think he just kissed me again, but nope, I truly am a geek. How else can I explain why his mention of science is a major turn-on? Steel waggles his eyebrows as if he realizes this too.

8

EMERSON

Here we go again. Like almost every Wednesday evening, April and I are at The Cloister, a student-run coffeehouse on Thatcher College's upper campus. During the day, the space is a typical coffee shop and study spot, but after dark, it's a catch-all lounge that hosts a weekly open mic night. It's pretty much the one regular social activity that I partake in at school, outside of class and eating in the dining hall. And I only do so because The Cloister is never crowded, and I'm addicted to their fried mozzarella sticks.

I don't have to go anywhere near the mic either, thank goodness! I leave that to April for her slam poetry readings. The theater crowd will often try out improv sketches here first, and the a cappella groups occasionally make an appearance too. Otherwise, it's mainly karaoke requests and people playing chess in the back. On Thursdays, The Cloister hosts monthly trivia nights, too, but besides the one Harry Potter challenge I won last year, I'm not the best at pop-culture details, which is why I stick to my science fairs instead.

We grab our usual high-top table with four swivel stools and wave to our hookup, i.e., the waiter Benny. He nods, jotting down our regular order in his notepad, and adds April's name to the performance list for tonight.

Perhaps my eye prescription needs an upgrade or I'm just plain seeing things, but for a second I could have sworn I saw our friend Jax in a back booth with campus hockey player, Luke Prescott, which doesn't make any sense. I know Diego and her are on the outs, but the "Ice Man" as he's dubbed isn't her type and vice versa. Actually, he steers clear of all relationship entanglements, at least that's what I've heard from the gossip grapevine. Look but don't touch, he's as cold as ice is what they say, thus the nickname. But when I look back at their corner again after ordering, the booth is empty. I must be imagining things or April's active imagination is finally rubbing off on me too.

Anyway, two eaten mozzarella sticks later, the very fine-looking Cal Chase spots us, or more likely April, from across the room and comes over at a trot. The senior track star always seems eager to run even when not competing. He kind of reminds me of a Labrador dog, eagerly bounding over to greet people.

"If it isn't Little Miss Sunshine." Easily a foot taller than her, Cal confidently places an arm around April's bare shoulders, but she immediately slips out from under his hold. I stifle a giggle because like her month-inspired name, April can be both sunny or stormy, depending on the day. Don't get me wrong, April is almost always pleasant around me, being her friend and all, but Cal seems to make her as grumpy as a grizzly. Yet, she's the size of a cub. It's pretty funny to witness, and apparently, Cal thinks so, too, his charming smile unfaltering despite her continued bites and snarls.

"So, *roomie*, didn't want to be home alone tonight?" Cal teases her with a playful wink. Crossing her arms, April mumbles something under her breath that I can't quite catch, but Cal apparently does and laughs, undeterred.

"Roomie?" I ask, interrupting whatever it is that they're doing—fighting, teasing, I'm not quite sure anymore.

"It's nothing," April rushes out to assure me. "The front door to my room is busted, so they had to unlock the connecting door between ours temporarily so that I can exit."

"And enter," Cal adds, then nods to me. "Hey there, Emerson! I hear you're old friends with my new bud, Steel?"

Again, with the 'friends' label being loosely applied to Steel Nash and me. The idea that the son of the most famous living rocker and I being friends or anything else is absurd, despite our teenage history. "We're just lab partners," I say, sounding defensive even to my own ears.

"Of course," Cal says, throwing me a wink now too. "Well, your *partner* is on his way, should be here any minute."

Hmm. If I leave now, Steel will probably see me

fleeing. No, best to stand my ground and then escape at the first opportunity. Good plan Em! Eat your food, clap for April and vamos!

"Yo Thisbe," Cal says motioning his head toward April, evidently referring to my friend with yet another nickname. This time though I'm clueless, but it sounds like something out of one of April's English literature novels that she's always carrying on about. "Foosball table is free. Wanna play?" Cal jabs a thumb over his shoulder, indicating where an empty table sits waiting takers.

April huffs. "What, none of your fan girls here tonight to entertain you?"

Cal glances deliberately around the cafe, then shrugs. "Guess you'll do."

"Ha, you wish!" April says, looking like she just sucked a lemon. "But … I suppose I have time to whip your ass before they call me up for my reading."

"Sounds like a good time to me," Cal says, mimicking an invisible whip being brandished with his wrist. I can almost see the steam releasing from April's ears, like an angry cartoon character. Yup, he's really stirring her up and I edge further away, just in case my tiny, yet fiery friend is about to explode.

To her credit, April ignores Cal's innuendo, and haughtily says, "You're going down, Chase."

"Oh, but I love to go down, Harris." Cal beams, before taking off to claim the table. As he races away, I hear him happily singing aloud to the lyrics of 'One Kiss,' which only seems to agitate April further. I shrug as I always liked the Dua Lipa song.

"Guy is too hot for his own good," April grumbles, pursing her lips as she watches Cal bound away.

"Meh, Steel is hotter," I say surprising us both. My hand immediately flies up to cover my big mouth. I can't believe I said what I was thinking out loud. I really don't know what's come over me lately or, rather, since Steel transferred here to Thatcher College, but I can't seem to keep my silly feelings private anymore.

April gasps, but I know it's not because of the completely unlike me admission. No, from the way her green cat eyes have doubled in size, and the familiar, spicy scent suddenly invading my senses, I know. I freakin' know Steel is standing behind me, overhearing me gush. Because why wouldn't he be? Seriously, I guess the universe just loves embarrassing me in front of him. No other way to explain the countless episodes otherwise. Yup, the universe hates me. Facts.

"Hi, Steel," April blurts out, officially confirming his presence before I can dig myself any deeper. As if that is possible.

"Hello," comes an all too familiar male voice that I can already tell is holding back a laugh. Just hearing Steel's smooth drawl close behind me has the hairs on the back of my neck standing with pleasure. "How are you today, May?" he teases, playing off April's name like the last time they met when he'd cleverly called her Wednesday.

"Another rhyme," April shoots back with humor in her voice. Oh yeah, they were rhyming then too, like they were reciting one of April's poems or something.

"Every time," Steel confirms with a nod. I shouldn't

be jealous of their easy banter and quirky humor, but I am as I continue to stand here like a deer in headlights. Say something Em. Be witty too, dammit!

"Sorry, but gotta go beat your buddy Cal at foosball. Shouldn't take long. Be right back," April says, heading off to where Cal is impatiently waving her over.

"Behave," I murmur, smothering a smile. I hope she wins because they could very well be playing here all night if not. I love her, but April has never been a good loser.

With my friend gone, I'm left with no choice but to finally acknowledge Steel. I turn toward him, already preparing myself. One dark eyebrow is quirked expectantly, but when he combs his hand through his silky, black hair, I lose my train of thought.

Words aren't needed as we share a moment of eye contact that feels way more meaningful than it could possibly be, considering I haven't even said hello yet.

"Hi," I squeak out, resisting the urge to facepalm. Yup, I should have remained mute. Unable to hold his stare any longer, I look down and notice he's clutching a wooden guitar. "Are you going to perform?" I ask lamely.

A brief flash of vulnerability lights his eyes before it's quickly gone. "Yeah, I was thinking about it," he says, sounding uncertain, glancing back down at his guitar too.

I'm shocked—not by the fact that he can play, but because he never once did while we were at Franklin Academy. With his dad being the famed Diesel, everyone kind of expected him to be in a band or at least show some interest in the music department, but he seemed to avoid it like the plague. Then again, Steel never likes doing anything that's expected of him.

Still, I always wondered if he played. I've been even more curious since Steel's biological discovery and learning he composed his dad's newest love ballad, which was so unlike Diesel's popular anthems. It happens to be one of my favorites, too, and that was before I knew Steel penned the lyrics.

Then there is the fact that Steel has a sexy guitar pick tattoo on the inside of his wrist. Hmm, I wonder if he has others. The thought has me once again drifting away in fantasy, and I shake my head to clear the annoying interruption. Now back to our regularly scheduled program of making a fool of myself in front of Steel.

"You should!" I tell him all too eagerly. "I mean, I could never do it," I add, pointing to my chest, "but April loves reading her poems here. It's a chill crowd, and everyone is always very encouraging."

His full lips twitch up into a smile. "I will, as long as YOU stay to encourage me," he says huskily. His invitation sends a jolt of exquisite pleasure through my body.

Gulp. "Why me?"

"Why not?" he asks with a shrug, like his request was no biggie, and perhaps it wasn't and I'm overanalyzing, as usual. "I need someone to sing to, you know, to focus on, and I'd prefer it to be someone I know. Only imagine how creepy it would be if I started singing to a stranger."

Creepy? Or every girl's wet dream? I can only nod, as whatever I was about to say, which I'm pretty sure would have been something like "humina humina," is interrupted by April, barging over and plopping down at the table to snag a French fry.

"Make way for the winner, if you please," she says, gloating and looking happier than she had only moments earlier.

"I let her win," Cal stage whispers, joining us, and April stiffens. "Glad you could make it, Steel," Cal says, extending his fist out to his new buddy, and the two do one of those bro fist bumps.

"Thanks for telling me about it," Steel says, bobbing his head.

"Wanna play foos?" Cal asks. "April here is refusing a rematch."

I don't know why, but I have a feeling Steel is going to refuse, it just doesn't seem like his sort of thing. Not that I know what is or isn't his thing. Fortunately for him, he's saved from answering.

"Steel Nash? Is the Steely Nash here?" a voice booms out on the microphone, and everyone seems to stop what they are doing to look around for the celebrity son in their midst.

"Guess that's my cue," Steel says, lifting his guitar and heading to the stage. When I say stage, though, it's merely a couple of wood pallets, a stool, and a microphone. "Another time," he mutters to Cal who bobs his head in understanding.

"Come on," Cal says softly, motioning his head toward the stage and for us to follow, and we do, temporarily leaving the table and our food. Claiming a spot stage right, we're standing only feet away, but we're not the only ones who moved closer for a better view. Mostly all of those who gathered are female. Go figure!

Steel sits down on the stool, looking at ease, propping one long leg up on the lower ring and cradling his wooden guitar as naturally as if it was his baby. Perhaps it is and I'm just discovering this passion of his.

"Hello," he says softly, leaning toward the mic, not needing to adjust it like April always has to by lowering it a foot. Several girls yell "hello" back, like they know him, but I guess everyone knows *of* him or at least his dad.

"This song goes out to Powers of Steel," he says, his dark eyes turning to lock with mine once again. Despite the gasp lodged in my throat at his secret dedication, I manage to give him a smile and a supportive nod. His lips twitch up into a brief smile, and my heart aches in a way that almost overwhelms me. Even though he's several feet away his quiet, intense stare seems to close the distance between us and has heat rushing over my skin.

Strumming his guitar, it only takes the crowd a couple of seconds before they recognize the song he's playing as Diesel's recent love ballad, the one Steel wrote himself. But he's doing an acoustic rendition. It's much slower, and with Steel's slightly gravelly voice, it's hypnotic, and wow, so much better than the rock version where you can't hear the beauty or meaning of the lyrics. From the murmurs around us, I think the crowd is disappointed he's not rocking out like his dad though. I'm not. I'm mesmerized. His voice is even sexier than his infamous father's and is one hundred percent his own. My heart races, beating faster than the tempo he's set. And even though I can see his hands and lips moving, he hasn't broken his eye contact with me.

"Wicked. Did you know he could play too?" April whispers in my ear, and I jump. I'd forgotten that she was here. That anyone else is here.

"He also wrote the song," I inform her, hoping I don't sound too annoyed at my dear friend's interruption. When I gaze back at Steel, he's now looking at the neck of his guitar and the placement of his fingers. I miss the intimacy of before.

"Really? He's a writer too?" April questions, and I'm not loving how impressed she sounds, and neither does Cal, given how the always happy-go-lucky dude is suddenly scowling.

"Hmm," April adds mulling over her own words and drawing out whatever she's about to say next for dramatic effect like usual. "You know … the girl in the song sounds a lot like you, Emerson."

"Don't be ridiculous," I mutter, wishing April will drop it and stop making my heart leap with unsubstantiated hope. But I should know her better by now. April isn't one to drop anything. We all have that friend, the one who always knows when you're keeping a secret. And that's my BFF April.

"Powers of Steel?" she muses, "as in Emerson Powers, and Steel, the guy who is practically serenading you right now?"

"Nooo," I say, drawing out the word testily. "As in the name of our future children's band." Oops.

"Your what!" April sputters just as Steel is ending his song, causing her exclamation to be heard by everyone around us.

Double facepalm. I can feel my cheeks heating, but April shrugs off her faux pas like it happened to someone else. I wish I could as easily. Standing, Steel chuckles into the microphone, and the crowd shifts their focus back to the stage, belatedly giving him a round of applause and I join in.

April dutifully claps, but her eyes are on me, demanding an explanation. Well, tough, she's not going to get one. Pivoting on the heels of my sneakers, I leave her and head back to our table, but the tenacious chihuahua is right on my heels.

Turning to face the music, so to speak, I tell her, "It's just part of our science project, ok?" But April shakes her head. Brat. "How about you let this go, and I'll forget about your new roomie situation."

April cocks her head, considering this for a moment. "Throw in one of your mozzarella sticks and it's a deal."

"Deal." I shove the half-eaten basket over to her and she daintily selects one, dips it into the cup of marinara, then spins away from me, heading toward the stage with scribbled notes in her hand. "Good luck," I shout.

She turns around with a smirk, giving me a knowing look as Steel leaves the stage with his phone and guitar in hand. "Good luck to you, too, Em."

I need it, especially when I see a new text lighting up my phone.

STEEL

Ready for the first item on your 'up to no
good' list?

Slightly panicked, I glance around the room. Steel is waylaid midway between the stage and my table. Naturally, a group is around him, but he's looking down at his phone and still managing to nod at something someone is saying near him.

Taking a deep breath I respond back.

I think so…

Think?!?

Let's do this!

that's more like it!

Meet me at 4:30 a.m. behind the hedges
outside of the student center

My head shoots up from reading his message only to discover Steel smirking from across the room. OMG what did I get myself into? And with Steel of all the dudes on campus or on this planet for that matter. You're not ready for this Em, no matter what you put on that stupid college wish list of yours. You blind fool.

9

STEEL

Dude, don't laugh. Just don't. Contain yourself.

But … nah, I can't help it. At least my laughter is quiet when Emerson joins me just before dawn at our meeting point, behind the hedges outside of the student center. She's dressed head-to-toe in black and slinking around like she's a cat burglar avoiding a minefield of laser beams or something. I'm surprised she didn't have us synchronize our watches before bed or use secret call names. One-Two-Papa-Papa-Over!

"Hey Slick," I whisper once she reaches me, providing her with a code name anyway. It seems apropos given the tight, black leggings that are molded to her sinful body, emphasizing her legs for days. My mouth is dry, imagining just how I'd like to make her "slick." My stomach growls, and it has nothing to do with it being four in the morning and not having had breakfast yet. It's because I'd love to be feasting on Emerson right now instead of simply imagining it for the millionth time. I dig my fingernails painfully into the palms of my hands to calm my raging lust. It doesn't help.

"Steel." Emerson finally acknowledges me through gritted teeth, while rubbing her hands together to keep warm. "I get why we are meeting early, but not why you'd pick the evening of the Leonid meteor shower. Half the campus is out and on their way to the sports fields. It's where I should be too!" She casts curious eyes up to the dark sky, but it's still too early to see the celestial event just yet.

"You just answered your own question," I explain, already enjoying myself just because Emerson is here next to me. "No one will expect for you to be anywhere else but in your bed at this hour or out seeing the cosmic debris. And thanks to the extra students around, it won't raise any eyebrows if we're spotted in the camera footage later."

Emerson's face pales and her eyes go alarmingly wide at the mention of security cameras. "Don't worry," I'm quick to reassure her. "There aren't surveillance cams here, but there is one pointed on the path toward the fountain. So, simply stay close, like we're two lovebirds strolling out to look at the stars." I'm a little surprised when she doesn't argue about the lovebird part. Instead, she nods, scanning the area as if to confirm that I'm telling the truth about the cameras. "See? Aren't you glad you brought me along for this scheme?"

I don't quite catch what Emerson mumbles under

her breath, but I smirk just the same. I'm probably better off not knowing.

"Do you have the stuff?" I ask, sounding like a drug dealer in the movies, which is very different from real life, and I should know. I never once met my dealer in a back alley. No, my connection operated via text and delivered my order from a bulletproof Cadillac Escalade. I don't miss those days. I'd much rather be sneaking around with Emerson for a silly campus prank any time—especially when she's dressed like this. She's the only drug I need to feel high. Aight, that sounds corny, but it's true. I literally feel the same drugging euphoria by simply looking at her.

"I have it right here." Smiling triumphantly, Emerson holds up a clear container of liquid that's no bigger than a bottle of shampoo.

"That's it?" I ask, unable to hide my doubt. "That doesn't seem powerful enough to produce the kind of effect we talked about."

"Don't worry, I made it myself," she says sounding superior, and it's a major turn-on. "It's highly concentrated. This one bottle is the equivalent of three jumbo jugs of the strongest laundry detergent you can find. Besides, the output of bubbles will only increase as the fountain continues to churn the formula, essentially doing the work for us while we slip away into the night."

I don't know why I'm impressed, as I expected nothing less from the brainy beauty before me. Still, it's fun to test her. "And … the bubbles won't start overflowing until we're out of there, right?"

She nods with a sideways grin that I very much want

to trace with my tongue and then down her elegant neck to suck on the pale flesh exposed. Picturing it has me groaning inwardly. *Simmer down now, Steel!*

Her eyebrows draw together, and she's poking her tongue in one cheek in thought. "Yes, we should have about fifteen to twenty minutes before the party starts," she informs confidently, totally unaware of my real thoughts and the party for two I'd rather be having. "We can expect the max results just in time for morning classes. Even those coming back from stargazing should be wading through some of the foam too."

"I believe we have a new prank master," I say, smartly placing an arm across my midsection and bowing to her for further emphasis.

Emerson inclines her head like a royal highness would do upon a loyal subject, and we both smile at one another. She's clearly enjoying this little bit of mischief, and it fills me with pleasure to witness it.

"Let's go make it rain up in here," she says, mimicking a DJ announcer's voice and throwing what I assume she thinks are gang signs, but it looks more like a surfer's hang-loose greeting. I laugh out loud, and she's quick to cover my mouth with her delicate hands, as if trying to shove the sound back into my person. Still laughing, I lick her palm and she jumps back, immediately releasing her hands like I knew she would.

"Don't play with fire, baby, or you're going to get licked!" I point out, and despite being in the shadows, I can see her eyes roll. "All right, let's do this, Slick," which I'm just realizing rhymes with lick.

"Save the rhymes for your lyrics and the licks for

your guitar," Emerson says sounding proud of herself, then stills suddenly. "Hmm … I don't usually do that."

"Lick?"

"No, enough with the licking," she says, swatting my bicep. "I meant, I don't usually say what I'm thinking like that."

"You could have fooled me," I tell her. "Remember that time I said you smell good? And you replied, 'Thanks, I use both nostrils.'"

"Yeah," she grumbles, looking down at the ground in embarrassment, a faint blush on her cheeks. "I only say stuff like that around you though. I guess you bring it out of me."

I hope to bring out a lot more than that, but unlike her voiced musings, I keep that point to myself. "And you bring out a better me," I say softly.

Emerson's distracted gaze shoots back to mine, alert once again. "What did you say?"

"Nothing." Taking advantage of her moment of shock, I pull her up alongside me. Unfortunately, not for the kiss I'm picturing, but to start our walk toward the copper fountain that holds the statue of Athena, the Greek goddess of intelligence and battle strategy. How appropriate.

Emerson squirms to get loose, which only brushes her breasts against my ribs, causing the air to catch in my lungs. She stills for a second and then tentatively holds on to my arm as we exit from behind the greenery and onto the path to the fountain. Walking almost in time together, her arm relaxes and slips around my waist to rest on my hip. It feels natural and not like we're pretending for the sake of a prank. And with the way Emerson is leaning comfortably in my embrace, I wonder if she feels it too. I could continue like this for miles, but we only have a few more feet to go.

"When we get close," I whisper, "look up at the sky, and I'll block you from view as best I can while you pour in your concoction."

Emerson scrunches her nose and nods before I bring us to a stop just near the lip of the fountain's circular edge. We both look up at the stars in unison, and then our eyes lower to each other's. The air is sizzling between us, every one of my nerve endings standing at attention. Among other parts. Without a chance to think it through, I lean in to capture her lips, but she's already rising on her tiptoes and meets me halfway.

The first touch fires an electric jolt of lust through me, from my mouth straight down to my cock. The clean, fresh scent of her overpowers my senses, and I thrust a hand into her hair, letting myself forget she's only pretending, that this isn't real, and I lose myself in the kiss. In her.

It's as if we've kissed a thousand times before, not just one time. It's effortless, and I can't get enough! And when I hear the tiny moan that escapes her throat, it's all I can do not to pull her down to the ground and devour her like a snack.

Remembering why we are outside in the middle of campus in the first place, I rein myself in, but it's not easy. I can barely hear my own thoughts over the pounding of my heart echoing in my eardrums.

With her eyes still closed, I gently dip Emerson back

like we're on a dance floor performing a waltz. "Go ahead and pour in the soap, Slick," I whisper against her mouth, not wanting to pull away completely. "You're right over the edge."

Emerson's eyes snap open and she nods, rubbing her lips over mine again as she does. Dutifully, she drops the arm she had slung around my neck earlier. I grasp her waist, and she extends her body gracefully like a ballerina, emptying the contents of the bottle into the fountain. When she's finished, I pull her upright and back against my chest. For a second, she stares at my mouth again, but just when I'm sure she's about to kiss me, her breath hitches and she points upward. "Look!"

I follow her gaze and catch a brilliant streak of light flash across the dark sky. We stay locked together for another couple of minutes, looking up at the meteor shower above us. It's magical. As clichéd as that sounds to my own ears, this moment is pure magic. One I know I'll never forget and not because of the falling stars, but because I'm falling for Emerson.

Closing my eyes, I make a wish on a star that she's falling too.

10

EMERSON

"You made a list?" Jacquie asks aghast, scooting her chair closer to our dining table in the upper campus food hall.

"Yes," I hiss back in my defense, but some things are too embarrassing to admit, even to your best friends. "Obviously, in hindsight I regret it, so there's no need to make me feel worse."

My other friend April throws Jacquie a reproachful look. "Sorry," Jacquie says sounding contrite, but her eyes are still alight with curiosity.

"I always make lists, and it made sense at the time. A sort of pep talk, if you will," I try to explain. "And it was supposed to be for my eyes only!" But now … my list is a reality, fantasies in motion. At least some of them.

"It's all anyone can talk about," April says before loudly biting into an apple.

"My list?" I exclaim, almost rising out of my seat in panic.

"Noooo," April coos, reassuringly laying a hand on my shoulder. "Your prank!"

"The unexpected foam party," Jacquie chimes in, and I'm able to breath normally. Now if only my racing heart would calm down too. "It's a college memory that no one will forget."

Me included. An image of being huddled against Steel under the stars flashes upon my mind. I can almost smell his manly scent and the taste of his warm, soft lips. My resulting sigh is not lost on the ever-perceptive April, though, and she eyes me with suspicion.

"You know, Cal swiped a lunch tray from the cafeteria and surfed down the pit of suds you two created," April says, sounding impressed.

"The neighbor we're not supposed to talk about?" I ask, hoping to give April a taste of her own medicine, but she only gives me a pointed, don't-go-there look. I back down immediately, not wanting to poke the bear further. Considering she hasn't teased me too much about Steel or my list, I better lay off, but at least I know I have ammunition to fire back at her if needed.

Jacquie clears her throat, breaking our silent standoff. "So, what's next on your list?"

"Party on Greek Row," I supply.

I haven't told them about the sexual wishes I'd listed out, as I'm not that open with my friends, at least not when it comes to private stuff like that. I just don't like people knowing my business, which is why it's weird to think that Steel knows more about me in that respect than my two college besties. Hmm.

Again, I'm picturing his kiss, and there's an

unexpected ache of longing in the pit of my stomach. Feeling his eyes on me somehow, I glance around the crowded dining hall for Steel. He's not there, but it's at that moment I realize I'm both anxious and excited to see him again. It's a confusing combo. Annoyed, I shove my plate aside. My nerves too shot to eat more.

"When?" Jacquie asks, bringing me back to the conversation and away from thoughts of Steel's touch.

"This Saturday."

"At Theta Kappa Gamma?" Jacquie asks enthusiastically. "I'll be there with Diego!"

Ugh. Somehow, I control my grimace. Knowing my friend will be in attendance only increases my nervousness. Because if I'm to make a fool of myself, I'd rather it be in front of strangers.

"Jax dragged me shopping," April adds, referring to Jacquie, the fashionista of our group. "You could borrow one of the dresses she forced me to buy. It's unlikely I'll wear them anyway."

"I might just take you up on that," I say, not having a clue what to wear Saturday, as I hadn't gotten to the outfit part on my to-do list yet.

"Oh," Jacquie says, bopping up and down in her seat. "We can do one of those TikTok try-ons, and my followers can vote for their favorite one."

"No!" I all but scream. Jacquie might not have a problem sharing every moment of her life to random people online, but nope, that's not me. I prefer to be the one scrolling through videos, not appearing in them.

"Will you give it up, Jax?" April says, clearly on the

same page. "I wouldn't do your movie montage idea in the dressing room yesterday either."

Jacquie sags in her seat and gives us both a surly look that tells us we're lame. I'd love to support my friend, but it's a hard pass for me. "I'll film you doing one instead. How about that?" I say, trying to placate her because while it might not be my thing, I know Jacquie truly loves executing the latest video trends. She's good at them, too, whereas I can't even manage the most basic dance steps.

Mollified, Jacquie blows me an air-kiss. "Thanks, babe. Now tell me more about Steel. Is he sexy like his dad?"

I shrug my shoulders. Poor Jacquie has no idea how loaded her question is—one she's forcing me to reveal—that yes, Steel is sexy as sin, but does he look like his dad? I don't know. Not even Steel can say who he even is.

"Yes, but in a different way," April supplies before I can. Her contemplative tone sounds like she's given it some thought, and for some reason, knowing she's been thinking of her brief encounter with Steel has me irritated. I should be used to it though. Every female at Franklin Academy was in love with Steel. And I know if I confessed that I had a crush on Steel, April would back off, but I'm too chicken to do it. *Had a crush or have, Em? Oh, shut up!*

"Go on," Jacquie urges, looking back and forth between April and me. "I need more details than that, or are you going to make me track him down and get a good look for myself?"

"All right, all right," I say, trying to placate her. She's so outgoing, I know she'd have no problem finding a way to do just that. "Steel is … well, he's a mix of contradictions. Rugged but also pretty, he has a swimmer's body, but isn't an athlete, confident but somehow vulnerable. He has gray eyes like a stormy day, yet they can also be sunny and kind. He'll make a stupid joke one moment and then say something soul searching the next. He's been through a lot, but he's come out okay. He's tough but not macho. To tell you the truth, I doubt anyone really knows who the hell Steel is, even him."

I look up to find my friends gaping at me.

"Well heck, and here I thought April was the poet," Jacquie says, her eyes giddy.

Damn. I guess I should have just left it at yes, he's sexy. This whole saying what I'm thinking habit has got to stop, and I blame Steel for it. I never had a problem biting my tongue before he walked on campus. Stupid Steel, bringing out all these emotions and thoughts.

Just great, and now April is peering at me like she's reading my mind again. "Seems like our Emerson has finally found someone who's caught her interest. And here I thought he'd never show."

Jacquie beams. "Yup, look who's catching all the feels!"

Catching? Ha, little do they know I "caught" those the moment I first saw Steel all those years ago, but it doesn't mean anything. He's just an insanely attractive guy. Who's heart wouldn't skip a beat at one of his devastatingly smooth smiles?

"Does he like you?" Jacquie asks, all too eager to gossip.

I shake my head. "We're just lab partners."

April snorts. "The chemistry between them is explosive," she says, nodding to Jacquie. "He's into her."

Now it's me who snorts. "I'm not Steel's type," I admit, realistically knowing he's simply flirtatious with every girl who crosses his path. Right now, he doesn't know many people here, but once he does …

"Opposites attract!" Jacquie declares.

"They call it an ionic chemical bond in chemistry," I mutter, nodding my head in consideration. "Ions have either positive or negative charges, and the different charges complete each other and fill the spaces that the other may be lacking."

There is a long pause until April says, with a chuckle, "Well, there you go. You can't argue with science."

I disagree. "This isn't a scientific debate. Steel likes women who are the complete opposite of *ME* not him … you know, models and other musicians."

My friends are quick with their compliments, but they are, of course, biased and simply being supportive. I'm lucky, but I'm taking what they say with a grain of salt.

"Girl, you're hot. You just don't flaunt it, you know?" Jacquie points out encouragingly. "Hell, if you just showed the slightest interest in any guy on campus, they'd be pawing at you in seconds." This really shouldn't delight me because who wants to be pawed at, but it does. I want to be groped, ravaged, kissed, you name it, especially by one particularly lethal guy who shall not be named.

"Not to mention you're smart and together," April adds, leaving me feeling shallow for my current dirty thoughts.

"Thank you, but in the end, he's a bad boy and I'm … a good girl." I hate to admit the former, but it's true. Even once I complete all the experiences on my list, I know I'll still be the careful and logical Emerson I've always been in the end.

But my friends won't let me fully board the negativity train. Jacquie is now singing the theme song from *Cops*, and April jumps in too. *"Bad boys, bad boys. Whatcha gonna do, whatcha gonna do when they come for you?"* Their teasing works, and I'm laughing too.

"And with your long, brown hair and blue eyes, you're going to look amazeballs in the cornflower-blue, bodycon dress that April bought," Jacquie says, clapping her hands like she's my own personal cheer captain.

"It's a Hawaiian luau theme," I point out, already regretting that I put going to a Greek party on my asinine list.

"OMG, that's perfect! We're going to get you laid!" Jacquie says, laughing at her own joke, and I choke from a quick intake of breath. April tries to come to my aid by smacking me on the back, but it only has me coughing harder.

Yup, if life has taught me anything, things can always get worse.

11

EMERSON

Entering the two-story sorority house, I realize the Theta Kappa Gamma party checks off every one of my expectations.

Music I don't listen to. ✓

People I don't know. ✓

The smell of beer and sweat. ✓

My anxiety at an all-time high. ✓✓

The dead pig roasting on a spit out on the front lawn was a surprise, though, not to mention seeing Steel in a Hawaiian shirt. Glancing at him beside me in the bright, floral shirt has me giggling. I've never seen him in any color but black, brown, and gray before. Steel groans when he catches me laughing at him, and it only has me shaking harder. He squeezes my hand, silently telling me to knock it off, but he doesn't let go after I've stopped chuckling, nor do I pull away. And that's how we enter the party—holding hands.

Surprisingly, having him near me, looking equally

ridiculous and uncomfortable, eases my anxiety and fills me with a confidence I normally wouldn't have. I'm not alone. In fact, I'm walking into the most popular sorority house on campus on the arm of the most infamous and hottest guy here. I only wish everyone from Franklin could see this. No, I take that back. New start, Emerson. New start. You're not the dean's daughter here.

Every head seems to turn our way as we push forward into the crowd. This is the bad part about being with Steel - the stares. I thought he'd be used to it by now, but he keeps scowling at the guys who look our way. Weird. He usually has no problem getting along with other dudes, even the frat types. Come to think of it, he's been acting odd since he came to pick me up.

I turn to Steel and straight-out ask him, "What's with you?"

For a change, his gray eyes aren't smiling when he looks at me, and his voice is flat. "What do you mean?"

"You're in a bad mood."

"No, I'm not," he says testily, negating his statement. I arch my eyebrow, letting him know that I call bullshit.

"Yeah, you are. Ever since I opened my door and you demanded to know where my glasses were."

"I was just surprised, that's all," he says, popping open the top button of his shirt and roughly adjusting the polyester collar. Despite his slim frame and the wild shirt, he looks as ferocious as a bouncer standing there, crossing his muscular arms. The slight stubble on his chin makes him look more rugged tonight too. Not to mention his viewable tats.

"Hmph," I huff. "And then you made fun of my outfit."

Steel jolts as if I pushed him and lets his arms fall to his side. "I did not! I only asked where you got that dress."

Remembering his displeased reaction when he first saw me still rankles. Why couldn't he have just lied and said that I looked nice? I try not to fidget or tug the bluish-purple, knit tank dress lower. April is several inches shorter than me, so the skirt keeps riding up my thighs. At least I didn't let my friends talk me into wearing heels too. I argued that flip-flops fit the party theme better anyway. Plus, I never needed the extra height.

Speaking of my gals, I spot Jacquie in the corner, arguing with her latest boy toy, Diego. Ugh, but I can't wait till she selects the next guy from her seemingly endless Pez dispenser of boyfriends. But another bad flavor always seems to pop up. Jax is so much more than she appears to be. I only wish she'd see that, too, and stop kissing so many frogs like she's trying to prove a point or something. Originally, I thought she was also hung up on someone back home, but she claims to be addicted to the early dating stage and none of the other entanglements. If you ask me, the beginning while thrilling is so damn awkward, but maybe that's just me.

I'm so busy observing my friend that I almost forget I'm at this party too and that this is supposed to be *my* wild night for a change. Right! Tonight isn't about her love life, but mine, or lack thereof. Just in the nick of time, Steel moves me out of the way of a drunk guy about to trample me in his attempt to catch a beer can being tossed his way.

"Hey, watch it," Steel growls at the oblivious dude, and I turn to take him in once again. The only time I've heard him sound as angry was when he punched Joshua on graduation day. Overall, he looks downright miserable being here with me. Great, so much for a fun time.

"I know this isn't on the top of your list, like it is mine, so if you don't want to be here, you can go," I tell Steel, gesturing toward the front door we'd just walked through. "You already did your part and got me in."

Shaking his head, Steel pulls me closer to his side by the crook of my elbow. "I'm not going anywhere," he says, locking eyes with mine. In that second, it's as if the crowd disappears and the music fades away. I blink and the moment is broken, my tunnel vision clearing. "Why don't I get you a drink?" he suggests.

Before I can agree, it occurs to me that this might be what's bugging him. "Are you okay with me drinking in front of you?"

Steel laughs, absentmindedly toying with the fake flower in my hair. "Everybody is drinking here. I'll be fine. It's good that I'm not anyway, so I can make sure that you're safe. That part was in parentheses on your list, no?"

I nod. To get drunk, safely. "And how are you going to ensure that?" I ask, and am surprised at how flirtatious I made it sound.

"By not leaving your side," Steel says, mashing me closer to demonstrate. His arm snakes around my waist and grips my hip, and all I can think is, harder! I want him to squeeze the shit out of me, and I'm dying to do the same to him. "I'll also fetch your drinks, and if you put one down, I'll get you another one. This way, you'll know no one has tampered with it, and later, I'll make sure you get home alright. Deal?"

"Hell yeah, that's a deal. Who'd say no to a drink servant?" I ask. Steel's lips quirk up into a grin, his mood no longer seeming so sour. "No worries though. Taking in my height and weight, I've calculated how many ounces I can have per hour without getting too shit-faced," I share proudly.

Steel's bark of laughter has more heads turning our way and I nudge him in the ribs with my elbow, but it's like ramming a closed door.

"Of course you did," Steel says, still chuckling. "Babe, I'm not sure math is going to help you. Everybody reacts differently. It also depends on what you're drinking and if you're mixing. And given the fact that you've never been drunk before, you'll need to deduct major points from your calculations for that."

"I already did!" I say, giving him a thumbs-up sign, to which Steel shocks me to my core by bending down and sucking my thumb into his mouth. Between his surprise attack and the heat enveloping my thumb, I'm too stunned to speak.

"I'll get you round one," he says, releasing my finger and leaving me there to stare as he heads to the inside tiki bar setup, near where Jacquie and Diego are now making out. That's one way to end a fight.

Steel is back in a flash, handing me a red Solo cup

with what smells and looks to be Jack and Coke. I'm relieved it's not beer.

"Beer before liquor only sicker," Steel recites as if reading my thoughts. "Figured we'd get this party started right."

I take a big swig and am proud that I hide my initial reaction to wince or make a face like a newbie. It's not that bad, so I take another sip or two, then three.

"Easy, chugger," Steel says, rescuing my cup from my hand. "We got all night."

I like the sound of that and the shiver that races through me.

"Anyway …," Steel says, mysteriously leading me across the room and out to the backyard, which is filled with tiki torches and an even bigger crush of people. It's a chilly fall night, but with the torches and fire pit going —and the many, many partygoers around us—it feels more like a cool summer evening. "We don't know what kind of drinker you'll be."

"What do you mean?" I ask, breathing in the wood-burning smell with delight.

"You know … like an angry drunk, the life of the party, or the absolute worst kind, a crier." He says this with a wince of his own. "Please don't cry."

I don't wanna cry, but the idea of making him that uncomfortable is rather appealing. "I won't," I reassure him, but really, I have no idea what's going to happen, and for once, it's thrilling. All I know is that I'm already having fun.

"What kind of a drunk were you?"

Steel grimaces. "An over-the-top one who'd do any stupid dare or challenge."

I bob my head. The stories I've heard confirm his self-observation. Turning my gaze away from Steel, I notice that the people outside aren't just milling about but are in the midst of a fierce limbo competition. Students cluster around the fringes, most of them with their phones up and chanting for the chapter president, Morgan Hyatt, to go lower. If she goes any lower, though, she'll be lying down.

"Are you game?" Steel asks with a suggestive wink.

I can hear the dare and my head is screaming "no," but for once, I refuse to listen. Forcing my social anxiety to the background, I down my drink and pass Steel my cup and stomp forward, next in line. When it's my turn, Steel is clapping and calling out my name. Even people I don't know are joining in. Gulping, I stand in front of the wooden pole, spread my legs the width of my shoulders for balance, and bend backward, inching forward with concentration. When I lift my head back up in a rush, it's dizzying. But holy crap, I did it! Everyone is hooping and hollering, and my heart is pounding faster than the EDM music playing. I'm about to turn to leave when the two guys on each end holding the bar lower it by two notches. Two!

"You can do it, Emerson," Steel calls out. It's the shot of confidence I need, but still, I'm doubtful. I haven't done the limbo dance since I was a kid, and even then, I don't remember being any good at it. Too tall and unskilled, but that was then and this is now. I kick off my flip-flops for a better grip, and the crowd cheers louder, watching the show I'm about to put on. I just hope it's a good one.

Focusing on each step, I bend my legs and back gradually as I see the stick ahead of me. Flattening my nervous stomach as much as possible, I begin to cross under the limbo stick. But it's too low, and my breasts bump into the rod. Wildly flailing my arms, I fall back, losing my balance, but before I can land on my ass, Steel scoops me up like I weigh nothing. The crowd goes wild, as if this was our plan all along. And instead of being embarrassed, I feel safe.

Now they are chanting "drink, drink, drink," but while looking up at Steel's dreamy face, I'm wishing they are saying "kiss, kiss, kiss" instead, like in some sappy romantic comedy. No such luck. Steel lowers me slowly, and I slide down his hard body, feeling each button on his tacky Hawaiian shirt skimming my skin. I notice Steel's eyes flare with heat, and I'm glad he still has a hand on my upper arm, or I might swoon like some silly girl in an Elvis documentary.

Before I can form another thought, the sandy-haired guy who quit our Advanced Bio class is standing in front of me, extending out a surfboard with three filled shot glasses glued to it. I barely catch the heavy board being shoved at me when the pretty Morgan Hyatt and a bare chested guy wearing a coconut bra and grass skirt join me. We each stand in front of a shot glass while holding on to the board together. The crowd counts down from three, and I'm left with no choice but to take the shot or have it dumped over my head.

I somehow manage to drink the entire shot of what I

think is Fireball without gagging. It's messy, and some of Morgan's drink splashes on me since she's shorter than I am, and only about a quarter of her shot makes it into her mouth. I wonder if she chose to wear a skintight, white bodysuit with no bra for just this purpose, though, because me and everyone here are getting an eyeful.

Hoots erupt around us, and Mr. Coconuts tugs my arm, pulling me over to where a band is starting to play instead of the DJ. Whipping my head around, I look for Steel, but Morgan is blocking his path and placing a plastic lei around his neck and a kiss on his cheek. Right. It's not like he's my real date tonight. And the purpose of being here is to be checking things off my list, which includes hooking up with a rando. And you can't get more random than grass-skirt guy and his rockin' washboard abs.

Shouting over the music, he leans closer to my ear. "I'm Allister Baldwin the third, but everyone calls me Trey." He reeks of liquor and likely has consumed more than just the surfboard shot we did.

I nod, shifting in discomfort, because his gaze has already lowered to my chest a dozen times in the five seconds we've been talking. "Hi, Trey," I say, smiling and accepting the drink he's holding out to me. Then he taps his cup against mine in an unspoken cheers.

Drink don't think Em! Most likely not the best advice I've ever given myself, but I'm not mad at it either. I don't recognize the libation, but it smells like rubbing alcohol, and I notice, from over the rim of the cup, a skeevy hickey on Trey's throat.

"Emerson, right?" he asks, circling my hips with his

arms while dancing alongside me. He pretends to do a hula dance movement with his hips, making his grass skirt sway, and I laugh awkwardly, feeling like it's expected and not sure what else to do. My stomach meanwhile tightens with disgust, not pleasure.

Calm down, Emerson. What's the big deal? He's cute, you're at a party, of course he's drinking and being stupid. Dance and enjoy yourself.

I close my eyes and sway to the music. It's only then that I realize I'm feeling a little dizzy and that my thoughts seem to be coming to me from far away.

When the song ends, Trey asks for my Instagram account name, only to sound annoyed when I say I don't have one, so he takes down my phone number instead like it's a huge favor that he's bestowing me.

"Come on, let's get out of here, beautiful. I live over at the track house, and there's always a party going on there," Trey says, his grip on my hip tightening, his palm sliding steadily toward my ass.

"She's not going anywhere, she came here with me." A deep, male voice cuts into our conversation and a large, masculine arm drops over my shoulders.

Trey scoffs, his hand tightening painfully on my waist. "Yeah? Well, she's leaving with me."

"Think again," Steel growls. I've never seen him look so menacing or as hot for that matter. Still, I shrug off both of their holds. I don't need a bodyguard. I was eventually going to say no on my own, once I was thinking straight.

Trey glances from me to Steel. "Whatever, dude," he says, scowling. "Emerson, I'll call you."

Before I can shake my head or plan to block his number, Trey surprises me by tugging on my hand and pulling me in for a brief, sloppy kiss. It's over before I can push him away, but it was long enough to know that I don't ever want another. Averting my eyes to the ground, I wipe away the taste of cigarettes and liquor with the back of my hand. Gross. It was nothing like Steel's kisses and guilt washes over me, which is stupid since I don't owe Steel an explanation. Besides, I didn't even initiate the clumsy smooch.

I'm forced to meet Steel's face when he unexpectedly pulls the cup out of my hand, sniffs it, and then pours it out onto the grass.

"Hey!" I protest.

"Did he give you this drink?" Steel demands.

I nod, knowing it was reckless of me. Steel curses and rubs a hand roughly over his face. "Emerson," he says, stabbing a thumb backward toward the retreating Trey. "You don't even know him, and you not only let him give you a drink you didn't see him pour, but you gave him your number?"

"Yes, but——"

"Come on, you're smarter than that. You should never accept a drink from someone you don't know, especially douchebags like that guy. And always get *their* number, don't give them yours. That way, you're in control and that way *you* decide if you want to call them or not."

He makes sense, but where has being careful and afraid gotten me? Nowhere! Taking a deep breath, I meet Steel's glare and shove at his hard chest, but he doesn't move an inch. "I don't want to be in control," I tell him. "I've been in control my whole life. That's why even the most basic stuff is on my stupid list."

Steel's puffed-up chest deflates, and his eyes soften when he looks at me. "I know," he says, sounding like he truly does understand me and pathetic me instantly feels weak in the knees. "I'm just trying to look out for you," he beseeches. "I can't take the thought of you being hurt or something happening to you."

Now if that wasn't the sweetest statement. Tears sting the back of my eyes and I'm afraid I'm about to break down, but the horror now reflected in Steel's eyes at my temporary emotion has me wanting to giggle. What a hormonal roller coaster.

"Whoa, come on, Emerson. What did I say about being a weepy drunk?" he says sounding horrified, and I sniff, trying to regain my composure before I either fall apart laughing or crying since both reactions are warring inside me, and I'm not sure which will win. "It's okay, you're okay. I'm sorry, I didn't mean to be so hard on you," Steel rushes out. Putting his hand on the small of my back, he all but pushes me back up the porch and inside the house. "Let's see if there's another limbo game going on or something."

12

STEEL

"Emm-er-son! Emm-er-son!"

My stomach cramps, a hot ball of something that's not jealousy slams me in the chest. It's the second time tonight guys are cheering her name, and I'm regretting my whole plan. I thought a weeknight sorority house party would be safer than a frat one, but I guess they are one and the same. It's wrong of me, but I was sort of hoping Em would have a terrible time, leave early, and thus allowing me to be the prince who rescues her away from her social nightmare. Except she's having a great time and was already kissed by some prick wearing a coconut bra. But I know it doesn't matter what the guy was wearing. I still would have wanted to punch him and every guy who has been eye-fucking her since arriving.

I also assumed she'd wear a Hawaiian shirt paired with running shorts or jeans like she usually has on. But no, Emerson walked out of her dorm room looking like a total smokeshow in a mini dress, a neon lei around her elegantly kissable neck, and a tropical flower pinning back her long hair. Not to mention the contact lenses. I always thought Emerson looked sexy in her geeky glasses, but without them obscuring her angelic face … well, shit! She's no longer merely nerd-hot, she's a volcano. I might as well have wrapped her in a bow because she's looking like a gift to every horny dude here. Me included.

"Emm-er-son! Emm-er-son!"

I mash my teeth together as I watch a muscular jock lift Emerson up under her armpits so she can place the final playing card on top of the astounding, science-defying house of cards that she's built. It's also the second time tonight she's given out her phone number. Turns out, she's apparently a trusting girl to everyone but me. The worst part is, I can't find fault in the current guy chatting her up. His name is Van something or other, and he seems nice, except that he isn't me and he's dared to hold her an extra minute or two after she placed the final, crowd-pleasing card. It doesn't help that I know exactly what he's thinking when he looks her up and down like he's doing now because I'm imagining the same dirty deeds. With each drink, she's gotten handsier, too, with me and any guy within touching range. Turns out she's also the best and worst kind of drunk—a flirty one!

This is what I get for making the mistake of leaving briefly to fetch her another drink. It should have only taken a minute or two, but Morgan waylaid me once again. I explained to the aggressive beauty that I'm here with someone, even if the *with* part is a loose definition.

Either way, she didn't seem threatened enough by Emerson to take me seriously, so I had to be blunt. Because that's where she is wrong. Emerson is the only one I have eyes for. I've accepted it, and she needs to also.

At that moment, Emerson's blue gaze, made even bluer from her dress and eyeliner, turns to me. Eagerly, she waves me over with one hand, while the other remains on Van's bulging bicep. Thankfully, she drops her hold on Van to extend an open palm out for her drink. Instead of the cup, I put my own hand in hers, and she twines her fingers through mine and my stomach does a similar twist. I shoot Van a get-lost look, and he heeds my warning with a shrug then leaves.

"It's a personal best," Emerson says, pointing back toward her card tower, which is still standing proudly.

"It's impressive," I say, brushing back her hair to whisper in her ear, "just like you." She shivers, and I tease her further by breathing closer to her eardrum, causing goose bumps to break out along her skin.

"Think don't drink Em," she slurs. "Or reverse that?"

Her mumblings aren't making any sense, but I'm encouraged when she sways toward me and nuzzles into my chest. When I look down, I see Emerson's eyes are dreamily closing. A second later, her weight crashes into me, and I have to hold her tight to keep her from dropping to the ground. Astonished, I realize she's asleep. Just like that. And in perfect timing, her house of cards collapses behind her as people cheer and toss the fallen cards at one another.

Grinning, I heft the sleeping Emerson off the ground and carry her out of the party. Guess I get to play the prince rescuing his fair maiden after all.

When we reach her dorm room, I knock on the door, hoping her roommate will answer, but no one does, even after I bang again, this time louder. For a moment, I stand there, holding Emerson, not sure what to do. Not trusting my control much longer, I refuse to take her back to my place, although I very much want to. As if on cue, Emerson's eyes drift open and close.

"Em, where are your room keys?" I ask softly. She moans and snuggles closer to me. If only she wasn't passed-out drunk, I'd be in heaven right now. "Emerson? Your keys?" I urge again with more force.

Dreamily, she slides a hand down from around the nape of my neck, dipping it into her enticing cleavage, where she fishes out a single, brass key and hands it up to me. Wow! I make a mental note to replay that little peep show again later when I'm frustrated and back in my own bed alone. It's about two a.m. now, so I tiptoe into her room in case her roommate is sleeping and didn't hear my banging. But both beds are empty.

I head to the tidier side of the room, knowing it must be Emerson's area. The photos of her parents and pile of science textbooks confirms it. As to be expected, everything is as neat as a pin. Even the dozens of checklist post-it notes that are stuck to the wall above her desk are organized in orderly, color-coded rows.

Gently, I transfer Emerson onto her bed. It's not my first rodeo putting someone to bed after too many drinks. I've done the same plenty of times for my dad and his mates while on tour over the years. Of course, it's a whole different struggle for me with Emerson, though, since I want nothing more but to curl up with her.

But my sleeping beauty sighs when her head touches the pillow, and I almost sigh, too, in longing. As if hearing my silent thoughts, Emerson reaches up and tugs me closer by my grabbing a handful of my shirt. Laughing, I fall next to her instead of on top of her.

13

EMERSON

STEEL IS HOLDING me at arm's length, but I want to be closer. Much closer. Oh, but this wet dream feels so good, except for the fact that my head is pounding and my mouth is dry. Wanting to stay forever in this state before waking, I nip at the nearest piece of flesh in frustration.

The resulting yelp I hear has me awake faster than if I'd been submerged in a pool of ice water.

Confused, I'm staring into Steel's laughing, gray eyes and look around to see that we're in my bedroom and on my bed. When did we get here? What am I doing? Panicked, I sit up abruptly, banging our heads together in the process. *Ouch!*

"What happened?" I ask alarmed, my head swimming and my stomach churning.

"Nothing," Steel says soothingly, sitting up as well. "You sort of crashed abruptly after winning a house of cards competition."

I rack my brain until memories and images start to form. "I remember starting to stack and place the cards, but that's it," I say, my voice sounding hoarse.

"You don't remember streaking through the quad?"

"What?" I choke out, feeling the blood immediately drain from my face.

"I'm only kidding," Steel says, biting back a laugh.

"Not funny," I retort, crossing my arms, to keep from hitting him for his teasing.

"Sorry," he says, looking contrite. "Nothing happened. You demonstrated your amazing card engineering skills, and then I got you back here safely," he amends. For some reason, this disappoints me. So much for my big party night of hooking up and letting loose. Seems like I needed a babysitter after all.

"Great, I fell asleep just when things were getting good," I mumble, combing my hair with my fingers. I probably look like shit, while Steel appears as handsome as ever, albeit goofy in his luau shirt.

Steel finds my statement funny, so I shoot him an angry glare, letting him know that I'm not happy about how tonight ended.

"Don't be mad," Steel says soothingly. "You were a big hit before that point. You even hooked up. so you can go ahead and cross off three experiences tonight."

I pause, remembering Trey, and grimace. "Yeah, but so much for number seven," I say under my breath.

Gasping, I cover my dumb mouth. I didn't mean to voice that thought. Yet, again, here I go, spilling out everything that comes to mind in front of Steel, who is smirking at me like he's indulging a little kid. Grrr!

Reaching out, he gently removes my hand and holds it between us. "Emerson, that's not how you want your first time to go down. It should be special."

"Oh yeah? And was your first time freakin' special?" *Don't tell me, don't tell me. Imaginary earmuffs activated.*

"No, it wasn't, as a matter of fact."

I hold my breath, waiting to hear more but, at the same time, not wanting to know. The former wins out. "Go on," I say, motioning my head for him to continue.

He sighs. "I was too young, and it was horrible."

Am I a bad person because I'm glad to hear that it wasn't good? "But … can it be bad for a guy?" I ask, wondering aloud.

He shrugs. "Technically, I guess sex is still good—even bad sex—but it wasn't how it should have been."

"Why?"

He pauses for a moment as if remembering it. "It just happened so fast. I was watching some movie at Joshua's house when he went outside to talk to his lady, and that's when his older sister kinda straddled me and we did it right there on the couch."

"But … but that sounds like every guy's fantasy, no?"

"I guess, but I wasn't expecting it, and … I was done too soon. It was embarrassing as fuck."

I burst out laughing and Steel winces. That's what he's complaining about? "Steel, but that's normal the first time."

"How would you know?" he snaps back at me, but without much bite.

"Everyone says the first time doesn't last long," I say,

patting his hand and soothing *him* now, realizing the role reversal has me laughing out loud again.

"Hey, stop it!" Steel says, giving me a teasing shake until I control myself. "Anyway, my point is that you don't want to regret your first time or cringe when you look back on it like I do. You should make sure you're with the right guy, someone who'll be patient and knows what he's doing."

He's looking at me so intently that I don't have time to guard my response. "Someone like you?" I gasp, hearing what I said. I must still be drunk.

Steel's head springs back as if I slapped him. "No!"

My gut clenches. I can feel the heat rising to my face and the dampness sprinting to my palms. Of course, he wasn't suggesting himself. Ugh, Em, why did you go and say that out loud? "Right, I know. I … uh … I was just kidding."

"No, let me explain," he continues, but I'm staring at the ground, hoping it will swallow me whole, which is why I'm startled when his hand gently lifts my chin up so our eyes meet again. "Drinking isn't the only thing that I'm done with. I'm done with casual sex too." When I don't bother to keep from rolling my eyes, he drops his hold on my chin. I can still feel the lingering warmth from his touch just the same. "I'm serious! I want my next time to mean something."

He sounds so earnest and so unlike the Steel I used to overhear, joking with his friends. No way is "hard as steel," which is what the many, many girls at Franklin who he used to hook up with called him, is giving up sex. Pahlease! Yet, he expects me to buy that, less than three years later, he's looking for something meaningful sexually. Ha! What he really means is he doesn't want to have sex with me and is only trying to sugarcoat his rejection. I'm not even worthy of a pity fuck apparently. This must be the new way of saying "it's not you, it's me." I cross my arms and give him a look that clearly says "now I've heard it all."

"Well, good luck with that and good night," I say tonelessly.

His pained expression turns to an aggravated one, but he's not leaving. He's clenching his teeth so hard, I notice a muscle flex in his rugged jaw. After a silent moment, Steel groans, and I feel that low vibration in my very center. "Emerson, please believe me when I say I'd seriously love to fuck your brains out. Really. Like so much, Em, and in so many ways, you'd need a brand-new notebook just to list them all."

Holy hell! His hot statement has my entire body flushing. I don't care if it's a lie because I know that's one list I want to oversee! Steel's hooded gaze lowers over my body, searing my skin. For an irrational second, I'm afraid my dress will melt away from his heated stare alone. And the cheap fabric I'm wearing is doing nothing to hide the fact that my nipples are hardening in response to his heated gaze and sexy words.

Immediately, I cross my arms over my chest. *Get a hold of yourself, and that goes for you, too, girls!* "Whatever. I don't need or want your help there, Steel, so you're off the hook for number seven."

I can only guess from the aggravated look on his face that this is the first time Steel has ever been turned down. Good, now that's one first I can have with him at least.

When I rise from the bed, it's too quick and my head spins. Still, I manage to point forcefully toward the door, indicating where Steel should go.

He doesn't.

14

STEEL

OFF THE HOOK?

I stuff my fists into my pockets in pure frustration. Of course I want to. Of course I want to be her first— her anything! The mere idea of someone else being inside Emerson has me wanting to smash a guitar. But I know there isn't an instant relief in this world that can erase the images now fluttering through my mind of someone else touching her, being between her long, lovely legs. Some stupid college prick who would use her, take her sweetness for granted, be rough, and move on. That's what most guys did in college, right? Not if I can fucking help it. Because if it can't be me, I'm for sure keeping any assholes away from her, like the grass-skirt douche from earlier. He doesn't deserve a girl like this. No one does. Especially of all, a screwup like me.

A girl who, at this very moment, is shaking her head furiously at me and pointing toward the door. A stupidly perfect girl who doesn't believe that I want her, when I'm ready to fall at her feet and beg for her body, her attention, her love. I'd give anything to have her turn those beautiful, blue eyes on me with trust instead of skepticism for once. I want her so badly, but for some reason, she thinks I'm not interested. I've gone and messed it all up like I always do. Hell, I'd be laughing if this was happening to anyone else.

Emerson shakes her head one more time, then turns away from me, spinning on her heel, her long, brown hair almost whipping my shoulder in the process. I catch her scent once again. She even smells sweet, like candy. "Christ!"

Tugging on her arm, I stop her from reaching the door that I know she's about to thrust open and shove me out of, but she needs to hear me out first. "I would give anything to do number seven with you. See?" I demand, pulling her wrist down and placing it over my jean-covered hard-on.

She gasps, and I grit my teeth to keep from whimpering when I harden impossibly more. I wasn't expecting how good the heat and the weight of her hand would feel even through my clothes. "Feel how hard I am just picturing having sex with you?" I ask, sounding hoarse to my own ears.

Her eyes are trained on the bulge in my pants and her own delicate hand covering my erection. She doesn't pull her arm away though. No, the infuriating temptress's fingertips slowly fan out to cover more of me. It's a tortuous pleasure, and it takes all my willpower to not dry hump her hand. Still, I can't keep myself from reaching out to grip her hips, which feel so fragile in my grasp. Her pert nose is scrunched in confusion, and it's so cute I want to kiss it. Yup, I want to kiss her nose. Do you even hear yourself, Steel?

I look down at her wide, blue eyes and I'm lost. There is no more self-control to cling to and no one to protect her now. Emerson opens her mouth as if to speak, but before she can get her words out, I lean down and capture her lips, along with a sexy moan.

If Emerson is shocked that we're making out again, she's not showing it. Her tongue invades my mouth, taking over the kiss. My first instinct is to take hold of her, mash her breasts against my chest, and grind my hips into hers, but somehow, I resist. I don't want to scare her away, but if she knew all the fantasies that I've had starring her, she'd be running for safety.

And here with me, in this moment, she is definitely not safe.

Just a kiss. Just a kiss will have to do, and no more. I repeat this to myself, hoping my raging hormones are listening. She's had too much to drink. No number seven tonight, big guy.

I let my hands roam her curves, and she is tugging on the buttons of my hideous shirt, pulling me closer to her wondrous mouth and bringing herself up against me at the same time. She's climbing me like the cat I likened her to before, but now I'm the one growling like an animal. Needing to memorize the feel of her, my hands are everywhere at once, eventually settling on cupping her rounded ass and lifting her off the ground and into my hold. She emits a squeak that I find delectable, and it only gets me hotter, which I'm surprised is even possible at this point.

My entire body stiffens when Emerson unexpectedly bites my bottom lip and then soothes it over with her tongue. Hot damn!

Twirling us around to switch positions, I take control, caging her lithe body against the closed door behind her, pressing the full weight of my hard body against her softer one. Possessively, she slides her arms up around my neck in surrender, and it's the sweetest offering I've ever received. Even as she gasps for air, I plunge my tongue deeper into her bewitching mouth, tasting, tormenting, taunting, heightening our kiss, our touch until I can feel myself leaking pre-cum like some inexperienced teenager. No, not like this, not now.

Tearing my mouth away from hers is more difficult than when I first turned away from drugs. But I know I can't quit her. Feelings, too many of them, clog in my throat. Dropping my head into the crook of her neck, I breath her in deeply. Spotting her racing pulse doesn't make me feel any better. Instead, I'm sagging back into her embrace to kiss the frantically beating spot and the tiny freckle next to it. I'm not sure who I'm trying to soothe, her or me, possibly both.

But … even though I don't want to, I need to leave, or I'm going to kiss the breath from her all over again. Still, for a second, I feel myself leaning closer, as if being pulled on an invisible string that leads to Emerson. Always.

Sagging against the door, she looks lost and helpless.

"You're even more beautiful than I imagined," I whisper almost reverently, placing a kiss on her forehead.

I put every ounce of feeling and desire in one more final kiss good night and slip out of her dorm while I still can. But all I know is that there is no way I'll ever—*ever* —be off Emerson's hook.

15

EMERSON

Several hours later, I wake up to three text messages from three different guys, which has happened … hmm … about *never* in my life. Plus, my room appears to be swirling before my eyes, and my tongue is stuck to the roof of my mouth. Getting out of bed, I remove the water filter pitcher from the mini fridge and flip open the top to drink directly from it, guzzling down H_2O like I just trekked the Sahara Desert.

Gingerly, I sit back down on my lofted bed and open my messages, now that I'm feeling a tad better. The first text is a "Sup?" from Trey, along with an eggplant emoji. I grimace, my stomach churning as I remember the slimy dude from last night. A drunken lapse in judgement on my part.

The second message is from Van with a humorous gif of a magician rapidly building a house of cards. I recall the football player being flirty, but a good guy at least, so I reply with a ha-ha tapback and leave it at that. The final one is from a concerned Steel.

> Morning, cutie! Try and stay hydrated today.

As far as I can recall, he's the only person who has ever accused me of being cute, and I grin down at my phone when another message pops up from him.

> Left you Gatorade and aspirin outside your door.

I bolt up from the bed and my bristling body punishes me for it, setting off a throbbing throughout my limbs, and I fight back the urge to hurl. More slowly now, I stumble toward the door. Opening it the smallest fraction, I peek into the bright hallway, wincing like a vampire in the sunlight.

Spying a paper bag on the floor, I grab the goodies and slam the door shut, resting my back against it. Just earlier this morning, I'd been almost in this same position while making out with Steel. Although then, I'd been dizzy for a much better reason. The memory sends a flutter to the pit of my belly, and my pulse races all over again.

Ripping open the travel-size packet of aspirin with my teeth, I swallow the tablets back without bothering to open the sports drink to wash it down.

Great, now I hear ringing in my ears too. Oh, wait, that's my phone. With a goofy smile tugging at my lips, I grab for it, assuming it's Steel checking to see if I'm following his hangover advice.

My smile disappears and I freeze, though, when I see my dad's photo on the screen instead. Sunday isn't one of our weekly call-in days, and my father always follows schedules, especially ones he sets.

"Hello?" I say, accepting the call and hoping it's not bad news.

"Don't you mean aloha?" my dad says, not sounding pleased. It's the authoritative tone he uses with his students and faculty, not me.

"Dad? What's going on?"

"I was planning on asking you that very same question."

A chill of panic runs through me. "What do you mean?"

I hear a huff at the other end of the line. "Let me tell you about my morning so far. It started with a Google alert with my daughter's name, which led to a link to a video of you doing the limbo in a barely there outfit that would never pass Franklin's dress codes, followed by you being scooped up by Steely Nash, of all people. What in the hell is he doing there with you?"

It's a lot to process, and my dad's play-by-play of last night has my heart racing double-time, but I'm not surprised he found out. His big-brother tactics come naturally to him. Given his headmaster status, he's been required to keep abreast of all the latest social platforms and spying techniques to keep "his children" safe. It's what the socialite parents at his school expect. And after he thwarted a student's suicide attempt due to cyber bullying, he's taken his social monitoring responsibility to the extreme. It's why I've avoided having my own social media accounts like the plague. "It was nothing, Dad. He—Steel," I amend, "is a student at Thatcher now too."

"And when were you going to inform me of this new development?" Ah, never. "And you're hanging out with *him*?" he asks before I can answer his first question, and my back immediately straightens at the way he says "him," as if Steel is scum.

"It's not like that. My professor assigned us as lab partners in Advanced Bio," I say, biting my lip and hoping I don't sound too defensive, which I know would only be blood in the water to a shark like my dad.

"Oh, so you *do* remember why you're there at college? And I suppose a frat party was one of your assignments?"

I'm tempted to respond that it was a sorority party, but again, I don't bother to correct my father. It won't get me anywhere except deeper in a hole. Besides, technically, going to the party *was* a self-assigned project of sorts, but I refrain from pointing that out either.

"It was only a campus party and we're friends," I explain lamely, hating that after only one minute into this call, I'm feeling like a minor again, carefully stepping around my father's big expectations for me.

And I realize…when was the last time I actually did what I wanted? I might have called my list stupid in front of my friends, but it's not. For once, I'm acting on my desires instead of stifling them like my family does.

I hear papers shuffling on the other end of the line, and I can picture my father, the dean, pacing in his home office with my mother silently listening to his ranting but unwilling to step in like usual. "Friends?" he repeats. "After all I did to keep you informed of his bad behavior when he was wrecking havoc here at Franklin? I'd assumed you'd be smart enough to stay away from him, but I guess I overestimated you."

Ooof. "That's not fair!" I exclaim, pounding a fist into my pillow. I've been damn near perfect—a model daughter—and I'm being crucified for one night of fun? I take a deep, calming breath before responding to his continued baiting. Drawing upon techniques learned from years of being forced to be on the debate club. I remind myself not to make the argument personal. Stick to the facts. "Believe it or not, Steel's been a superb lab partner. We received an A on our first project together."

"No doubt you did all the work," my dad says in clipped tones.

"That's what I expected, too, but Steel's changed. He's focused and dedicated. He's even competing for Thatcher's MBA internship competition and is already a front-runner."

"Oh, I'm sure he is. Emerson, do you know how naive you sound?" my dad asks, and I grind my teeth at his patronizing stubbornness. "Merely over a month into the school year, and you're under his influence—drinking, partying, and doing who knows what else."

"Steel doesn't drink anymore," I protest. "He's been sober for two years."

"And that's supposed to be some sort of comfort? A twenty-one-year-old in AA hanging out with my daughter? You know what else I'm piecing together? The other week, I read about Thatcher's fountain being defaced. That kind of behavior has Steel's handiwork written all over it."

"Actually, that was my idea," I confess proudly.

"Yours?" he sputters. "Lovely. Add destroying private property to his influence too."

The pride I previously felt seeps away, tainting a memorable night. "It was a harmless prank," I say, but it sounds so childish in response to his accusation.

"I doubt campus security or Thatcher's administration would agree. Keep this up, Emerson, and you'll lose your scholarship."

I gulp involuntarily. "I promise you, I'm still giving my studies 110 percent." I'm just giving my social life some much-needed attention too. Was that so wrong? I could do both successfully. Right? Yes, I will!

"You better be," my dad says, shaking my silent resolve. "Or forget about me paying for your housing next semester, instead you can go ahead and finish your degree remotely."

And be back under his thumb is what he really means. If the idea of losing my scholarship jolted me, it's nothing compared to this threat. Before I can find my voice, my dad ends the call without bothering to say goodbye. Now I'm really going to be sick. Who needs aspirin or a cold shower when my dad can sober me up with words?

I'm already sitting down at my desk and reviewing my class notes when my roommate enters, bragging about the crazy night she had at some townie bar. Like usual, she doesn't bother to ask about my evening. Why should she though? Normally, my answer is the same—

not much. Smiling to myself, I flip to the back of my Bio notebook and cross off Greek party and getting drunk.

Only two more to go.

What happens when my list is complete though? Do I cross off Steel too? I know that's what my dad would expect of me, but now I'm not so sure what *I* want. He's not the rock star's spoiled son that my dad has always made him out to be. No, he's so much more for not only surviving his father's fame and privilege, but thriving. To think that over a month ago, I never wished to see Steel again, but now that unpleasant thought has my stomach aching and my heart plummeting. I know it's absurd to feel this way so fast, but … but … it's almost as if I feel incomplete without him now.

I didn't tell Steel before, but I already put a line through "hookup" after our first kiss back in his room. I'm glad because I'd have hated for Trey's slobbery one to have claimed it instead. Soooo, if I feel that way about a bad kiss, how could I have considered doing number seven with just anyone? Nope. Steel has gone and ruined me. He's the only one I want as my partner, and I'm not talking about just for Advanced Bio.

But how can I tell him? How can I take that chance? I only hope that Steel's tendency to bring out my inner thoughts will guide me and that I don't clam up like I did with my dad just now.

Time to make a new list … and I'll call it my "No Longer Daddy's Girl" list. I'm grinning to myself as I start to write out a new plan.

16

STEEL

Fuck me. This isn't fair. My eyes are trained on Emerson's sinuously swinging hips like I'm some tennis line umpire.

Good girls aren't supposed to dance like this or have all these sneaky, hot dresses hiding in their closets. Tonight, she is wearing some sort of burnt-orange, long-sleeved number that reflects the subtle highlights in her rich, brown hair, which is down and flowing towards her ass, which is outlined and molded by the tight material. Her glasses are gone again too.

The front of her dress plunges low, and the bottom stops just above her thick thighs, while the sides have these mouth-watering, diamond-shaped cutouts, revealing her smooth skin and the hips I'm dying to grab. It's like the dress is instructing every bozo here exactly where their hands need to go, like a sexual Twister board.

Luckily, we have black, velvet ropes keeping any

admirers away, which is good because it's an older crowd here tonight, and the luscious Emerson isn't looking like she's still merely in college. My man, Augustine, got us into this hot, new club VIP style, skipping the lines outside along with the bouncer checking IDs. I doubt anyone though would question Emerson's age in this dress. We also have bottle service and a half-moon table all to ourselves, not that Emerson has sat down since arriving an hour ago. I've already been offered blow but declined it for a Red Bull and Emerson is sucking back her second long-neck bottle of some girly hard seltzer drink, and it makes my throat go dry each time she flicks her tongue out to sip from the cool glass.

"Is she a Diesel Guzzler?" Augustine asks me after pocketing the tip I've slipped him, along with the equally VIP ticket package for when Diesel performs at Fenway Park this summer.

"NO!" I shout, and luckily, Augustine thinks it's because I'm trying to be heard over the noise and not my revulsion after picturing Emerson as a Diesel Guzzler, which is the term for my dad's more dedicated fans. "She's a future chemical engineer," I say proudly and more calmly.

"No shit?" Augustine says, glancing back at Emerson, who has her eyes closed, her arms raised, and is gyrating to the DJ's vibing music. "She's definitely giving *me* a reaction."

Get in line. Thankfully, Augustine, who I used to like, leaves, and Emerson waves me over to dance with her. I'm there before I can nod.

Having danced before walking and sang before

talking, I pick up the rhythm quickly. It's a pulsating beat, and it has our hips popping close to one another. It feels like she's lighting a match on my skin every time our bodies slap and grind into each other. Seriously, do all self-proclaimed science geeks have moves that can rival a Coachella raver?

The music slows slightly, and Emerson twirls in front of me, then drops low and rises back up my front, twining her arms around my neck. Our eyes are locked, and as our bodies move together like magnets snapping into place, it's as if we're back out under the stars, or in my room, because it feels like it's just us right now.

Something flares in her eyes, which, in turn, makes my cock twitch. Sliding my hands into the side cutouts of her dress, I squeeze the silky-smooth flesh that has been teasing me for years. Instead of pulling away, she undulates closer. Does she know that her body is moving in that slow, sinuous rhythm, as if I'm already inside her?

She's wearing a sexy smirk that tells me, yes, she knows exactly what she's doing to me. Mmm … my turn to play. Protected by the fabric of her dress, I let my hands roam underneath it from her sides and around and down to her shapely ass. Shocked to discover she's wearing a thong, my eager hands are now full of her fleshy cheeks, and I pull her into me and the erection she's gone and caused. The primitive growl that rises from my throat can be heard over the loud beating of the music.

I'm likely leaving handprints from my grip, but good! I want to mark her like she's somehow done to me from the moment she shot her nose up in the air and pivoted away from me, her gorgeous, brown hair flicking perfectly in tow with her hips while she showed me around Franklin. Referencing terms and subjects that I'd never heard of before, and because of *her*, I became desperate to learn and become more than just being street smart. To prove myself. To her.

Of course, dummy! She's always touched something in me. Making me feel more, want more, wish more, like no woman has ever done before. This girl, who's currently dragging my face down to her mouth, and I dive in, capturing and tasting her lips, her tongue, like my next breath depends on it.

Gradually lowering down her body, I let my mouth and the stubble of my five-o-clock shadow trail down the line of her neck, through the valley of her cleavage, savoring each instant, absorbing each need, shiver, and longing. When I return up to her sinfully, gyrating body and back to her lips, her eyes flutter open, dazed and a darker blue than I've ever seen them before.

"Steel," she says achingly, gazing into my eyes. "Can I ask you something?"

Anything. It's at this moment I realize I would tell her anything. Bare my freakin' soul if she wanted it. "Ah …" Crap. Drowning in her blue eyes, I forgot how to speak. My heart is beating faster than a Diesel drum solo. Somehow I've got to convince her this is not pretend or about her list. She has to feel *this*.

"I guess it's not a question, but I—I want, but I just don't know how or what to say." She's looking up at me, imploring me somehow and I'm trying to follow, but I'm so lost in my own thoughts and feelings. "You're supposed to bring the words out of me." Sounding annoyed, she states this last part into my chest, where she's now burying her face.

Automatically, my arms come up to hold her. I can feel her melt into me, and it's like a freakin' salve to my heart. Yes, I've been crushing on Emerson for what seems like forever, but I didn't realize I needed her quite so much until this very moment, feeling whole just from holding her.

"What words, babe?" I croon. "What can I do, tell me and I'll do it."

Shoving away from my chest, she looks up at me, with fuck-me eyes and I almost swallow my tongue.

"Do *me!*"

17

EMERSON

Do me? OMG, did I just shout that in a crowded nightclub? To *the* Steely Nash, who is looking at me like I'm the three headed dog in the Sorcerer's Stone? I don't blame him. After all, I just ordered him to *do me.* WTF was I thinking? I wasn't. It's Steel's fault, too, filling me with such need. A need for him, both sexually and … well, with a feeling I've never felt before.

I want to run all the way back to campus. I think I could do it, too, and if I died along the way, that wouldn't be so bad either right now. As it is, it's likely going to be a long and very awkward ride back up to school.

Grabbing my clutch, I push past the stunned Steel, practically tripping over the rope I forgot was there in my attempt to dash toward the private staircase we came up earlier.

Steel tugs on my arm just before I can open the emergency exit. "Wait, don't go!" he says, looking bewildered. Why wouldn't he? He's chasing down a mad woman.

"I shouldn't be here." Club dancing was well and truly outside my comfort zone and being this close to Steel?

"You're right," he agrees quickly, and it feels like a punch to my gut. "You're too fine to be out in a club like this, and you're not leaving without me."

My snort can rival one of April's, and I throw up my hands. "Oh, come on, look at me."

"I am. I can't keep my eyes off of you," Steel says, his eyes roaming over my body, illustrating his point. "We need to talk." Tugging on my arm, he pulls me toward another door marked private. Hauling it open, a shocked Augustine inside starts to protest, but when he sees that it's Steel, he stops and puts down the walkie-talkie he'd been holding, placing it on the tiny desk he's leaning on.

"Sorry, Aug, could you do me another favor and give us a minute?" Steel asks his friend or contact or whatever he is. The room we just barged into is no bigger than a broom closet and smells just as dank. Besides the desk, there are dozens of security screens showing different viewpoints of the club.

"Dude, there is a hotel a block away," Augustine sniggers, leering at me.

Steel's grip tightens on my arm, and he levels Augustine a stare that could melt, well, Steel. "I just need a moment to call for a ride and a private place to talk, five minutes tops."

"I have to check in with the other VIPs anyway. Go

ahead and make it ten, you two," Augustine says laughing before shutting the door behind him.

Steel holds a finger up as if to stop me from speaking, which is fine by me because I have no words. I seriously haven't had any control of my mind or mouth since Steel stepped into our classroom this year anyway.

He finishes sending off a text to who the hell knows and shoves his phone into the back pocket of his painted-on jeans. "A car will be here for us in a few minutes, but we need to talk, Emerson, because our signals are getting crossed and I don't want to fuck this up."

"Fuck what up?" I ask boldly. Ah, look who suddenly has words.

"Exactly," Steel bites out, placing his hands on my shoulders. "We need to figure that part out right now."

"But how can I think when you touch me? I can't, don't you see?" I exclaim, shoving his hands away yet wanting them back at once. "I was just in the moment, okay. I didn't mean to shout that out there. So, let's not make a big deal about it, okay?"

"No OK," Steel says with a growl, but this time it isn't lusty like earlier, it's in pure frustration. "Emerson, please. I thought I made it perfectly clear how much I want to 'do you,'" he says using air quotes. "Hell, we were pretty much doing just that out there. I just don't want to be an item you check off on one of your lists."

"Why not?" I cry out. "You used to check off lots of girls' lists."

Steel shoves a hand through his silken, black hair,

and I can see he's just as confused and anxious as I am. "That was before."

"Before you were sober?"

"No, before you," he says roughly. "I'm here because of you, Emerson."

"I know … because of my stupid list. Well, you took me clubbing, thank you. Now I can cross it off my list and leave," I say, hands on my hips.

Steel lets out a long sigh. "Ugh, no, you don't get it," he says, pacing, but given the lack of space, he doesn't go far before turning back to address me again. "I didn't mean I'm here tonight at this club because of you or your list. I meant you're the reason why I'm even at Thatcher." Whatever I was about to say escapes on a shocked exhale. "I'm not rejecting you. I only said I didn't want casual sex from you," Steel says through gritted teeth.

"I don't understand. What *do* you want from me?"

"Everything!" he growls, and I see the heated look in his eyes and my breath catches. Reaching for my hips, Steel grabs me in his embrace, pulling me closer to the point where I can hardly breathe, except to inhale him in, but it's all I need. "I want *YOU.*"

My heart soars, his words sending a jolt of exquisite pleasure through my body. But this is a lot to take in. His frank honesty, the way he's looking at me, it just doesn't compute. "But … but why me?" I ask, tears welling up in my eyes.

Steel throws up his hands in a helpless gesture. "Damned if I know," he scoffs glancing up at the popcorn ceiling, like he's asking the angels for help. "No,

I take that back," he adds, holding me out at arm's length so he can look at my bewildered face. "You love lists, and *I* can list the reasons why. You're smart, responsible, beautiful, kind, witty, loyal, and passionate. You're everything I didn't know I wanted or needed, Emerson. You. We are connected somehow, don't you feel it? This is different. I see you and you see me."

I know one's heart doesn't actually stop in such instances, but the aching pang I feel in response sure seems like mine just did. And for someone who was generally ignored growing up, his words, the way he's looking at me, well, it's rearranging my whole perception of myself. Steel sees me. Has always seen the real me.

Steel opens his mouth to speak, but before he can get his words out, I stand on my tiptoes and kiss him with all the joy I'm feeling. Kissing me back, Steel lifts me off the ground, bringing me even closer. It's a different kind of passion than our previous kisses. This feels more intimate and not solely a sensual exploration.

"Sooo," I ask with a shy smile once Steel eventually lowers me back down to the ground, leaving me to stand on wobbly legs. "If I were to say that I want something more serious, not casual, would … I mean, could we hang out regardless of my list?"

"And here I thought you were the smart one," Steel says with an exasperated laugh. "Yes, you stupidly amazing girl. I don't want this to end. Helping with you list was just an excuse to be with you outside of class."

I nod, feeling stupid, like he just said. But oddly enough, I'm not embarrassed because even though I was slow on the uptake due to all these darn feelings he's stirred up in me, I have to know for certain. "Then we're agreed that experience number seven … it's going to be you?"

His teasing smile drops away, his expression turning to pure smolder, and it makes my gut ache with longing. "Hell yeah," he says, pulling me close and playfully smacking my ass in reprimand. "You're all mine. But let's do one more do-over and go out on a real date first, no pretenses, no tasks to tick off."

"Deal," I say, very, very much looking forward to it. Throwing him what I hope is a sexy, coy look, I point out, "Although I think you mentioned something about needing a new notebook …"

"Oh baby, I'll buy you a great big notebook to fill. I'm going to show you moves standing, sitting, horizontal, vertical, more ways to make love than you can count. Backstage, onstage, in a limo, mile-high club, oh, but I'm just getting started. I promise you're going to feel empty whenever I'm not inside you." Steel's hot guarantee goes right to my core, and I let my mind wander with fantasies. "Come on, let's get out of here because if you keep looking at me like that, I'm going to forget about our date and your first time is going to be here in this ugly office, which is not on my list of places for us."

Us! I like the sound of that, especially coming from his gorgeous mouth and dirty mind. Placing my hand in his extended palm, Steel smiles, and I know, beyond a doubt, these *will* be the best years of my life.

18

EMERSON

WHO KNEW bad boys liked to play hard to get?

Maybe not all, but this one is dragging out his seduction to the point where I'm unable to think of nothing else. I can't even concentrate on my studies and for me that is saying something.

But Steel is evidently made of actual steel because he doesn't just take me out on one date as promised, but three "proper dates," which is what he calls them.

The preamble for our first date started with an odd text.

STEEL

Find the out-of-place sticky notes up on
your wall.

Just the idea of something not in order had me rushing to my post-it wall of to-dos. The additions were easy to spot not being in an even row and in Steel's artsy scribble. The notes read: hat, gloves, scarf and thong. The last had me laughing, while the others puzzled.

He then greeted me at my door with a bouquet of sunflowers. When I asked him how he knew I loved the bright and welcoming flowers, he reminded me of the stickers I used to have on my binder back at Franklin Academy. I still can't believe I never noticed him noticing me. And not because he wanted to torment me as I'd thought, but because he was genuinely interested in me, but I suppose my own insecurities had refused to believe it. Although, Steel seems to have no qualms about tormenting now by kissing me breathless and then saying goodnight and leaving me wanting more.

But not before we'd spent an evening walking around the winter farmer's market and exploring the holiday festival in town first. While sipping hot apple cider Steel asked amusing "Would You Rather" questions. I know he was trying to get to know me better, but all it proved was we already knew a lot about one another. I guess I'd cataloged my share of Steel's interests too. My confessions left Steel beaming as he held my hand.

Then came a casual double date with Cal and April over at Pizza My Heart Italian Restaurant close to campus. While it was a lot of laughs, it was hardly romantic. Well, except for when Steel played footsies with me under the table when he'd reached for another cheese slice, looking as innocent as can be. At least I was able to blame my shocked gasp when he inched higher up my thigh on the cheese being too hot. Nope just me feeling all hot and bothered by my sweet tormentor.

Tonight, for our third date though, Steel outdid himself by taking me into Boston again. Not to go clubbing this time, but for a private tour of The Museum of Science led by the museum's Senior Curator no less. I could have stayed in the Project Vaccine exhibit asking questions for hours, but for once science wasn't the only thing on my mind. No, I was more eager for what was waiting for me after the tour – Steel and finally completing number seven on my list.

"After you," Steel says, holding open the door to a premier suite at the luxurious Mandarin Oriental on Boylston Street.

From the way the staff discretely greeted and checked us in without waiting at the reception desk only proves why so many 'A' list celebrities like Steel's dad choose to stay here. Likely it was costing him a small fortune for our one night stay too.

As expected, the room is opulent with creamy neutral tones, not expected though is the soft music playing and trail of red rose petals strewn across the carpeted floor leading to and on top of the king size bed.

Seeing my gaze riveted on the enormous bed with its abundance of pillows, Steel scrambles to reassure me, wrapping his strong arms around me from behind. "No expectations Em, we don't have to tonight, whenever you're ready." His voice, soft and sensual, sends shivers down my spine. Spotting my involuntary quiver, Steel teases me further dropping a kiss just below my ear and then traces the shell of my ear with his tongue. Turning in his arms I pull Steel down for a deep kiss that has him shuttering now too.

"Oh, I'm ready and I have a LOT of expectations after all this build-up!" I tell him, only half joking.

Steel snorts and shakes his head in disbelief. "You think you've been waiting a long time?" He asks, shoving a trembling hand through his hair. "No pressure, huh?" He says with a growly laugh, then scoops me up under my knees and throws me down on the feather bed. Giggling, I bounce from the impact.

When I lean up on my elbows, Steel is already over me, his arms braced on either side of my body. And boy the view is fine. He's sexier than any rockstar I've ever seen.

"I was contemplating booking an in-room couple's massage for us first," he confesses, interrupting my sex crazed thoughts, "but I didn't want anyone touching you but me."

Proving his words are true his hands are massaging my shoulders before restlessly brushing up and down my sides, leaving sparks of electricity along the way. Gripping my hips, he pulls me closer to meet his hard erection, which causes a hiss to escape his lips.

Wanting to both soothe and intensify, I lean up to capture his mouth and our tongues dance an ancient rhythm that has me undulating under his hard frame as I sink my hands into his dark, silky hair and sigh.

"I'm going to try my best to take it slow Em," he says, "but you're so beautiful and you feel so damn good." His voice is deeper than I've ever heard it and it sends a thrill through me from knowing I'm the cause. I do this to him. I affect him this way.

Moaning he buries his face in my neck and drags the skirt of my dress up and over my hips. The rasp of his day-long stubble scrapes my neck, and the resulting sensations sends liquid pooling at my core.

Our kisses are wild, frantic, and our bodies break apart only long enough for me to tug off his shirt and for him to slip my dress off over my head. Surprising me with his quickness, he snatches the cups of my bra and drags them down so that they rest under my exposed breasts, raising them up high despite lying on my back.

Groaning Steel leans down to bury his face between the valley of my breasts and now I'm groaning too when he twists his head to brush his lips slowly along the sensitive sides. Gradually he makes his way to my nipples, which are puckered and hard as he starts to suck on each one in turn. Circling them with his hot wet tongue he finally takes the tips between his lips and sucks my flesh further into his mouth.

My hands that were stroking his hair are now reflexively tugging at the strands and gently scratching his scalp as they open and shut due to the onslaught of sensations rippling through me. When he abandons my nipples, I want to cry out in objection, even as he trails delicate kisses down my torso to the top of my drenched panties. I lift my hips silently encouraging him to remove them, but his lips curl into a sexy smile and he drags his nose down the seam of me, breathing in my arousal through the fabric. When he lifts hooded eyes back to me, they are filled with a gleam of lust that I never dared hope to see. Oh, but how I crave it. How I want more.

Reaching between us, it's my turn to tease and I cup his erection through his pants. He pushes forward into my palm, and I trace the outline of him with my fingers.

"These need to go," I order, but Steel is already nodding and getting to his feet to remove them. He kicks them off with annoyance when they get stuck around his ankles and huffs out a breathy laugh. Shooting me a just-you-wait glare he is back in my arms in a flash. A naked flash.

Finally, Steel hooks his pointer fingers around the straps of my panties and slowly drags them down over my knees, slipping them off my legs. Instead of flinging them like I expected, he throws them on top of his head like a hat and we both laugh. Smiling, he brings his face back down to the apex between my legs and my eyes go wide. I'm not sure how much I can take before I demand that he fuck me already and make our bodies one, but for now I can only moan as he parts me with his tongue and places a firm but quick kiss on my clit, only to replace the wicked touch with a flat, slow lick, lapping me up.

He alternates between sucking, grazing and tracing circles on my swollen clit causing me to buck my hips off the bed. But he grips my thighs and pulls me closer to him though, letting one palm trail up my stomach to capture a breast before trailing back and behind me to scoop my ass and center me even closer to his mouth. When he slides his hot tongue inside me, I'm clasping and twisting the bedcover like a heathen.

"Oh, damn Em, you're so wet and sweet." He adds two fingers between my snug walls and asks a question he already knows the answer to. "Are you ready for me?"

"God yes!" I demand and he breaths out a husky laugh and places a quick kiss on my forehead before collecting a condom from the pocket of his discarded pants. I'm so relieved that he isn't leaving that part up to me that I relax further into the mattress.

Steel positions himself between my legs and enters slowly. I can feel myself tighten, bracing myself for an onslaught of pain, but it doesn't come. And when Steel is fully buried inside me, I sigh underneath him in relief.

"Are you okay?" He asks, worry clear in his tone as he looks down tenderly into my face, his arms straining to keep himself upright.

"Yes," I rasp in wonder. "It doesn't hurt," I assure him. I'm so wet and excited that it's true. Yes, I'm full to the brim, but it's not uncomfortable, it's just right. I'm relieved too, because although I didn't tell him I was nervous, I was an anxious ball of nerves. But I had no reason to be with Steel, because like he said it should be, this is special. And he made it so.

Smiling, I nudge him with my hips, wrapping my legs tighter around his waist. That's all the encouragement Steel needs before pushing in and out of me in an even more delicious rhythm than our kisses danced earlier. We're so lost in our frantic movements that we almost fall off the other side of the bed. Steel has to haul me closer and rolls us back to the middle to keep from toppling off.

A knot of tension builds low in my belly with each

of Steel's strokes inside me and when he leans up like he's doing a push-up and angles his hips so my clit receives the onslaught of each of his thrusts, the friction is just what I need.

I can feel him in every part of me and when my orgasm hits, the intensity has my head swimming. Steel isn't far behind, and I can feel him pulsate inside me as he groans his release, then pulls me closer and rotates us to our sides.

In the aftermath we are a sweaty mess of tangled limbs and heavy breathing, and I'm tracing lazy doodles on his chest like I do whenever I'm distracted in class. Usually during those times I'm of course thinking about Steel.

"Well?" He asks between deep breaths of air.

"It was perfect," I assure him with a quick kiss. He tastes like me and us.

"Perfect?" He echoes, his smile wide and cocky now.

I nod. "How are we going to top it?"

An arrogant laugh rumbles through our entertained bodies. "Remember that notebook we need to fill? Well, give me a few minutes and we'll get started on topping perfection."

"You know," I say dragging the thought out. "There is no such thing as a perfect science, but… I've never failed a test yet."

Steel barks out a happy laugh and I've never heard a more perfect sound.

"That's my overachiever," Steel says with a smile,

which he then transfers to my own lips with a soul-filling kiss.

EPILOGUE

EMERSON

EXAMINING MY LIST TITLED "LIVING ROOM," I spot one last unchecked item.

"Air purifier?" I call out to Steel. Dutifully, he pokes around the labeled boxes and suitcases piled about in our new, one-bedroom apartment, walking distance to campus.

We signed the rental agreement last week, just in time for our final year as undergrads. Although, if we like it here, we'll likely renew since Steel is all but guaranteed an acceptance into the MBA program. And with my new intern-to-hire position at the biggest pharmaceutical company in New England, I'll be hanging around here too. Bonus: If I agree to work for them for two years, they will cover the tuition for a master's degree. I would love to earn my PhD, too, but we'll see where life takes me ... *us*.

Between what I saved up during the summer and the minimum wage I'm earning from my campus internship, I should be able to contribute my half of rent too. Not that Steel asked me to, but it doesn't seem right otherwise.

Diesel had generously offered to buy Steel his own place, but he managed to talk his dad out of it for the time being. Although there were not-so-subtle hints about it being a future wedding present, but neither of us are ready to go there yet. It's been great watching the two of them become even closer ever since the DNA revelation. It took some time, but Steel wisely came to the realization that "A dad is someone who raises you and loves you, so he's my dad no matter what." His exact words. And while Diesel can't be more different than my father, he's very caring and managed to look interested during my nervous rambling about the neuroscience behind music and the impact on the mind.

Steel continues to rummage around the room and I bite back the giddy smile I feel about to bloom. It's funny to see Steel being so domestic, but I think he's been enjoying nesting even more than I have. He grew up on the road so much, I'm eager for us to have this place together, even if it's just for a year or two. I don't even mind the guitars he's mounted on the walls or the history lessons he gave about the significance of each one while he hung them up. It's endearing to see him geek out for a change instead of me. He's also on the fifth book in the *Harry Potter* series now, and while not a full Potterhead like me, he's enjoying them. Guess I ended up with a fellow geek after all. He's just been disguised as a sexy badass all this time.

Come to think of it, I've learned that while opposites

attract in science with every magnet having a north and a south pole, in reality, though, people tend to be attracted to those who are similar to themselves, as dozens of studies have shown. I just didn't realize how similar Steel and I were until I scratched beyond the surface, combined with his help in unearthing my own inner bad girl. Or perhaps more accurately, we "complement" one another. It's the hypothesis I'm working on for my senior thesis, and once again, I have the ideal study partner to help me with it. Smiling to myself, I watch as Steel continues his search for the air purifier machine while humming the new song he's working on for Diesel titled, "Powers of Steel."

The absolute best part about finding a place off campus is we're able to live together, no roommates, and my parents can no longer hold paying room and board fees over my head either. My dad, true to his word, cut me off in that area, but despite his fears I've maintained my GPA and scholarship, so he couldn't make me come back home either. As for Steel and I living together now, he of course isn't happy about it, but tough! He can't expect to control me forever. But man, you should have seen his face when I brought Steel home for Christmas or when he visited over the summer vacation. That's a mental image I won't soon be forgetting. At least by the end of the summer, they finally seemed to have warmed up to each other, albeit begrudgingly. Poor Steel. After putting up with him, I'm not worried about us living together. That should be a piece of cake in comparison.

"Aha, found it," Steel finally says, holding up a white

cylinder and cord like it's a trophy. "Where do you want it, ma'am?"

He's been playing the part of my butler for the last hour, and not gonna lie, it's pretty nice. "On the ledge by the window, if you please," I say, pointing with the pen I'm still holding. "They say it should be at least three to five feet off the ground and in a place with the highest airflow."

"But of course, ma chérie," Steel agrees, now sounding like the candlestick in *Beauty and the Beast*. As he probably intended, it has me giggling.

After he plugs it in, I say "check!" and gladly cross it off. "That's it for this list," I inform him with a smile, making my way toward the couch with the notebook in my hand. "Break time!" Truthfully, I'm hoping for a little Netflix and chill action, and by the grin tugging at Steel's lips, I have a feeling he's thinking the same thing.

Before I can plop down on the battered, but comfy, brown sofa, Steel holds up a hand to halt me. "Are you sure that's all?"

Did I miss something? Frowning, I glance back at the list, running down the column with my finger, but am relieved to see that yes, everything is checked off.

"Turn the page," Steel suggests, sitting smack down in the middle of the couch, propping his bare feet up on an empty box where eventually a coffee table will go. Leisurely, he spreads his arms out, taking up almost the entire space.

My eyes narrow, knowing he's up to something. "There's nothing on the back," I tell him, sounding offended. I would know. I carefully wrote each item, and

I flip to the next page to prove it. I do a double take when I see a new entry written in Steel's handwriting. It reads, "Love Steel."

Now how cute is that? I can't even describe how much I love him. All I know is that I feel closer to Steel than anyone else in my life and frankly I can't imagine not having him in my life.

Looking into his smoky eyes, I straddle his sprawled legs, and as I slowly position myself in my intended spot. Looking into his eyes, I happily cross off his request. "Check," I say, sitting on top of him, teasing him a bit by rocking gently back and forth, then left and right on his lap. His arms go from being stretched out to wrapped around me before I can settle into place.

"You really lived up to your name, Steel," I tell him, grinding harder.

His deep groan vibrates through me. "How so?" he asks distractedly, nipping at one of his favorite targets, a freckle at the base of my neck.

"Because you *stole* my heart."

Steel squeezes me harder. "Prove it," he says against my ear.

"I will," I agree with a sigh, intending to do just that for a very long time.

Want more Emerson & Steel?

They both appear in *Hot and Cold*, the next book in the Lesson in Love series.

HOT AND COLD

CHAPTER ONE

Jacquie (Jax) Silva

From the stares and snickers trailing in my wake, you'd think I was the first teapot to ever walk across Thatcher College's beautiful New England campus.

Alright. Yes, I just heard what I said. Muttering to myself like the lunatic I must appear to be, I pick up the pace and force myself to hold my head up. But all this seems to do is cause the bulbous costume I'm wearing to wiggle about my waist further and lift the protruding spout higher into the air. So yeah, I probably look even more like a kettle that's about to boil over.

Here is my handle, here is my spout. When I get all steamed up, hear me shout—

As if reading my thoughts, some dude passing by calls out the last part of the nursery song, "tip me over and pour me out," and his group of friends fall about themselves.

Ha, ha, you're so clever. But I'll be the one with an

extra $375 in my pocket at the end of the day, thank you very much. Granted the added humiliation was a bonus I wasn't counting on when I agreed to this campaign. My own stupid fault though as I was supposed to change into this getup once I was safely over at Diego's building and after I helped him with his film studies essay. Then, he said he'd record my paid TikTok idea for a new online tea subscription service that is sponsoring me.

Which was all well and good, but then I had to go and try on this monstrosity ahead of time and ruin my whole plan. I just figured if I practiced the choreography while wearing the costume, it would cut the number of takes required later. Except … when it came time to remove the awful thing it wouldn't budge, no matter how I wiggled, jumped, and rolled around on the floor of my dorm room. I think the clasp must be stuck to the black bodysuit I'm wearing underneath it. And of course, my roommate isn't here to help a girl out.

I'd managed to sneak down the Tasker dormitory stairwell and outside to my car with minimal attention, but before I could pat myself on the back, I belatedly realized driving over to the sports house where Diego lives was no longer an option. I only wish I figured that out before I struggled to stuff myself into the front seat of my Kia only to have the costume ride up around my face, blocking all visibility.

After resembling an experimental performing artist exiting a clown car, I accepted the forgone conclusion I was going to have to walk the mile of shame to Diego's instead. It was either that or rip apart the teapot, which

I have every intention of doing, but only after I get my skit recorded. Then, all this humiliation and frustration will be worth it. Almost.

So, despite the early November chill, I'm sweating bullets in this getup as I waddle across the courtyard and wave jauntily at yet another cell phone being lifted to record my misery before shuffling up the steps of the two-story colonial home on the edge of campus. I've actually never been inside the building despite the fact that I've been sort of seeing Diego, a soccer player and fellow junior in my film studies class. Then again, it's more like we've been hanging out nothing official. We've gone to a few parties together, which Diego considers "dates," and he even tagged along with my friends to see the Leonid meteor shower last week, but honestly, I think we're nearing our expiration date.

Thank you, next! That's been my relationship motto and I don't care what anyone thinks. I've never been one to make a quick purchase, so naturally I've been trying out different guys like I do the outfits in my popular fashion try-on videos, which got me this influencer gig to begin with. My fashion fails especially do well and I'm hoping this absurd teapot bit will bring me to the attention of other brands that may want to collaborate. Cha-ching!

Diego has been supportive and patient with my video requests, even gladly appeared in one. Although, I think he enjoyed the attention he received in the comments from my followers more than wanting to help me out. Kind of like our so-called relationship, we seem mainly for show. Time to shit or get off the pot as my granny would so eloquently say. Or teapot in my current state. I snort, proud of myself for still being able to make a joke right now.

Heaving a breath of relief, I rasp my knuckles on the wooden door, hoping Diego will answer and not one of the two dozen other athletes that live inside the catch-all sports house. After a moment of standing there like a fool, I knock again, more forcefully. That's right, I've never claimed to possess the virtue of patience.

What feels like an eternity later, the door swings open and I'm ready to stuff myself through the doorway and out of sight, but all I can see is the wall of a man's chest blocking my way. Glancing slowly up, a long way up, I meet the coolest blue eyes I've ever seen.

Although we've never met, I know the icy stare belongs to none other than Senior, Luke Prescott, a.k.a "Ice Man." A nickname given to him not only because he's the captain of Thatcher's legendary ice hockey team, but due to his chilly personality, hard as ice body and equally as thick … ego.

Well, Ice Man, step aside, because this teapot is ready to spill the tea.

Now Available!

* * *

ABOUT THE AUTHOR

Blogger and former PR executive, Tara holds a master's degree in Journalism and Communications from New York University and a B.A. in English from Wheaton College in Massachusetts. For 

Nineteen years, she has penned a popular lifestyle, travel, and parenting blog at TaraMetBlog.com.

An avid romance reader, she has been daydreaming about being a romance author since high school. Dozens of bad dates and adventures later, she still finds it impossible that she met her husband on a New York City subway. Now they live in sunny Southwest Florida with identical twin boys and four distractions (I mean cats) underfoot. When the kids are asleep and the cats are not lying on her keyboard, she's finally writing the happily ever after tales she's been dreaming about.

www.TaraSeptember.com
@TaraSeptemberAuthor